Robbie Hughey

CRISPY FRIED
AND
SOUTHERN BROWN

Southern Humor

Jimmy Washburn

Bloomington, IN   Milton Keynes, UK

authorHOUSE®

AuthorHouse™
1663 Liberty Drive, Suite 200
Bloomington, IN 47403
www.authorhouse.com
Phone: 1-800-839-8640

AuthorHouse™ UK Ltd.
500 Avebury Boulevard
Central Milton Keynes, MK9 2BE
www.authorhouse.co.uk
Phone: 08001974150

First published by AuthorHouse   5/10/2007

ISBN: 978-1-4343-0755-2 (sc)

Printed in the United States of America
Bloomington, Indiana

This book is printed on acid-free paper.

DEDICATIONS

Dedicated to the lady of my life and the woman I love. Dedicated to my two children who have given me a cause to love and prosper through the younger years. They with my life's special partner have held me true to the course and made my life worth living. If you knew these three people you would find the semblance over and again throughout this book. Not in the form of scorn or mockery, but as honest everyday sweet people.

I also dedicate this book to the true Southerners who will in their big-hearted way, read this material and laugh along with rest.

Let us not forget my two secret loves Nancy Travis and Cathy Stephenson. They have given me the unreachable!

May God Bless You All.

Contents

INTRODUCTION

Alert readers will find areas in this book that will have no similarities with any other book on the market. Not written to match or sound like that of any writer except maybe a remote resemblance to the writing of Lewis Grizzard.

Written as comedy, but not all-comic literature. Some as solumn predictions and questions that deal with our own identity as part of the human race and as spiritual beings. References to God and the Bible will be as real as ever though not given in chapter and verse.

The South is a bit different in accepting the world and her events yet at times sounding a bit comical. They are a people who have always accepted life in a layed back manner, finding some fun in about everything including the gray areas.

Did you know that everything below the North Pole is South. All the way back around to the starting point is South even though some call the trip up the back of the world North, but to us it is all South. For this application however, we are going to refer to the Mason Dixon as a starting point and go to the bottom of North America.

So find a shady tree, hang the hammock, crawl in for a rest and take this book along for a companion. Have a fun afternoon engrossed in its colorful rendition and in your own drowsy way.

I hope you will become involved in this Southern critque and find laughter, not directed at the people, but the semblance bestowed upon us in times past.

CHAPTER ONE
The Consensus Is

The South has always stood on it's own, which is an excellent sign of Independence. The South has always became defensive and very aggressive when their rights or beliefs were infringed upon. The South has always believed in their God and their Country, until the last few years anyway. They know their God created the Earth and no other way will be tolerated or accepted. They have always known that the Earth is six thousand years old and not <u>one minute more</u>.

They know that Jesus came upon the Earth two thousand years ago and through him is the only route to heaven. They know that the Earth is not billions of years old, because there is just not anyone on this earth or under it that is old enough to prove it. If there was someone on earth that was old enough to prove it, he would be so wrinkled that his eyebrows would hang down over his eyes and he would not be able to see his calculator. And his wife, what a wrinkled ole girl that would be, put Olay completely on top in the business world.

Now we believe that anyone not believing the way we believe are absolute nuts. Evolutionist do not believe there are any absolutes, but they are not absolutely sure. See, didn't I tell you?

Evolutionist are not really sure about anything except that they are tax supported.

Southerners are changing some in later years, a small per-cent of them are trying to become civilized, like city folk. A few of us are clinging to the true Southern ways and bringing our children up in the tried and true. Some of us are still beginning our male children at five to study the mechanism of the American fire arms and teaching them to be crack shots, just in case. We have no intentions of getting caught with our britches down again, no matter what the cause or reason. Oh no!

There are some who are trying to become involved in the politically and socially correct and are using terms that most of us have never heard of. There is getting to be a lot of name calling going on, family feuds, and one serious beating over this correctness movement. I think that it's sort of like a bowel movement, not sure.

I guess everybody has got to be doing something and some just to be noticed. After all Southerners hardly ever get their name in the papers.

Our beliefs are alive and well and are becoming more widespread. I have heard that they even go as far north as Indiana, I hear that quite often. If they keep going it won't be long until we will be able to take over the North and never fire a shot. But ain't that Communism or some kind of nism.

I am thinking that the biggest problem with taking over will be the retraining. Making Southerners out of the north people will be trying and very expensive. At that time we of course will be open to suggestions.

Making the North a southern country will be a task like Abe Lincoln taking on the job of trying to make black white and white black. Someone is going to get the idea that it might be easier to teach the, other people how to live together without fighting. That ain't going to be an easy job either. If people could just quit being so picayunish and consider the advantages of living together without fighting.

I knew a man once who had two dogs a boxer and a Chihuahua. The boxer didn't like the Chihuahua at first, but every time he tried to attack the Chihuahua the little rascal showed how fast he was by darting in and biting the boxers leg, same leg evertime. Then after it swelled to the size of a large zucchini squash the Chihuahua would choose another leg until the were all so sore the boxer could hardly get around. Finally the boxer got the idea that it would be a lot easier to make friends than to fight, since he was gaining no ground anyway. Now where one goes they both go the best of friends.

Of course that wouldn't make any sense for two countries, do you think, I don't know. Nah! Besides it would be hard for Bush to bite the Iraqi leaders leg that often with their itineraries as full as they are.

We could do like Switzerland, we could become neutral and build a force so tough and expediant that no one really wants to up set them. They go out of their way not to rile the Swiss or Australians. We could stay out of other peoples business until things went far enough to draw us in regardless, and this hasn't happened since World War II. I don't think!

It appears that an army being a widespread broad opponent is not much of a problem for the ole US of A, but these dudes that stay hid all the time are becoming annoying. We may have to send a group of country boys over there and straighten them out or kill'em.

I know killing is not a very popular thing in America, unless it's an unborn child. Americans don't seem to have the gut for it their opponent has or just don't have it anymore at all. Either that or the war has just become so profitable that certain groups can't allow it to stop, yet. However, I know some politicians are going to keep on letting it go on until they are going to make the majority of the American people mad enough to do something about it.

The Americans still remember who owns and runs the government when it comes down to brass tacks.

Bush don't seem to realize that his tenure is about over, but there is still time to get caught with his britches down. Of course it will not be the same as it was with another of our presidents. He was caught with his britches down so often people began to think that was just the way he wore them. I heard a man say once who lived in the city of Clinton, Arkansas, that a man really had to be full of himself to have his State Troopers pick up a certain lady and bring her to his office and as soon as she walked through the door to just drop his trousers to the floor. I said, Aw man you're lying to me! He promised me he wasn't, but I find that HARD to believe, don't you?

If every time some countries had a disagreement we would just keep our nose out of it, upon coming close to the stage of complete annihilation, they probably could find a common ground. Seems like every time we want to flex our muscle just a little we get into someone elses dispute and then it becomes a conflict and when we realize they are not going to buckle under because of our big muscle, it becomes a war.

If I remember correctly when we finally did begin to address the drug problem here in the USA the advocacy was to teach them the need for another approach. We began by starting classes, strict reproach for those breaking the laws and to rebuke any new actions abusing these laws. We were looking for ways around putting them in prison, putting them to death, or killing off family lines. Rafe McCutson was overheard asking the question, " Did they really mean that?" He also said, " that you can lead a horse to water, but you can't make him drink, but you don't kill him for it.

Why can't we be satisfied with big brother instead of, brute force daddy. Big brother is a big thing in the south, we attach ourselves to a younger person and try teaching him through our actions. We take them places and let them see how we face the world, how we find solutions to our daily problems and how we sensitively suggest Christian living. Sure sounds better to me than sending a plane over and blowing them off the map.

When are we going to understand that we are not scaring them, just killing them. Other countries don't automatically start shivering at the mention of the United States. We have been looked upon for years as a leader, as a teacher, as a Nation with cunning and a debonair way of approaching life. We have been seen as a professor in business and creating a better way. And God has been lenient and supportive to our initial cause. Things are becoming different now and your guess is as good as mine, but God won't let it go on forever! Now you can take that to the bank! As a friend of mine says, " that'll preach."

God made us big and leaders, and he can reduce us to small potatoes, again. Or we could be reduced to a pile of burning ash, (which ever comes first) with the very equipment that we wish to war with. It would be wise to look further into the idea.

Everyone makes light of the Christian view of the world, but we are just going by what God told us. We get our information from the Bible, what folks are calling just an old fogy history book. Well that ole fogy history book says that one day the eastern sky will split with a great noise (which will be the only real big bang theory) and Jesus Christ will appear to carry his children home and every knee will bow and every tongue will confess. Do you know what that means, TOO LATE.

P.S. Did you know that the only reason that the North won the war between the North and South was because the Southerners were just too soft hearted? They just didn't have the heart to shoot all them Yankees!

CHAPTER TWO
The People

We have a lot of different kind and a unique people here in the South, like anywhere else of course. I can't tell you about all of them, because I don't know them all. But I can tell you about the ones in our local homeland. Each state area they say has it's own unique culture and I suppose that is right. Some have been known to make cheese, buttermilk and yogurts, but without it we would just get lazy.

I want you to keep in mind that we are talking about the South here and: Southerners have a knack for keeping up with everyone in their hometown, some even call them busybodies. We have our own busybody and I ain't never seen nobody as good at it as Mrs. Myrtle Martha Mitchum. She will put a piece in the local newspaper every week. She will talk about the churches, businesses, neighbors, sick people, stick people, poor people, mean people and their animals. Talk about a busybody Myrtle Martha is one of the best.

There are a few very important people in our town and they don't like to be talked about, but you know how that is? There is Billy Bob Hagnot, Bubba Joe Pierce, Letha Ellen Switcher and Ella Mae Pfleuger. There is one other lady in town that is not as important as the rest, but everyone knows her.

Lila Emma Ruth is a very well known person. She has been to about everyone's house visiting, even eat at some of them. You know what they say about the South, "if you're hungry, we'll feed you". Lila is a sister to Dr. Ruth and she too is a sex doctor. She is also a sex fiend and I think they both go together, I'm not sure.

I hear Dr. Lila Ruth is a very good sex doctor, because when the townsmen call her and tell her that they are too sick to come to see her at her office, she will make house calls. They all seem to perk right up after her visit, brings them right out of it. They are usually back on the streets by night. Lila is not a bad looking woman either, but her hair is always a mess.

Billy Bob Hagnot is the towns mayor, a very lean and learned man and self-taught. Billy Bob can put a plan together before you can say his name. He saved the town once from complete destruction, bankrupt it twice, but pulled it out of the red both times. He is a money magician if there ever was one. It seems strange that Billy Bob was the only one to make any money from his schemes.

Me, Thelma Lou Abernathy and Rose Jean MaCrack were the only ones in our town to have a college education. All the rest were self-taught and man I really admired them for their guts. They all thought we were aliens and didn't mind telling us about it. Bubba Joe once told Rafe McCutson an Irish import, said that we were just outcast coming to the town functions and such.

Thelma Lou came back to town with her newly acquired education using big words all over town. Them big college words scared the living daylights out of most common everyday people. She was talking to Bubba Joe one day and used the word facetious. Nearly Killed Bubba Joe, he ran all over town trying to get some insights on the word facetious. He told Rafe, "that he knew what a face was, but in spite of all he could do, he just could not figger out what a <u>tious</u> was. Said he even looked in the Webster dictionary and nothing there".

Rafe McCutson, now here is a rare breed, probably the smartest man in town, but he thinks so himself. He told Rose Jean Killary on a date one night if it weren't for those damned college people he would be the smartest man in town. He said he had studied hard to become as educated as he is and those college people ruined it for him. He even accused us of being sort of like having Yankees in town.

Rafe the only teacher we have in town like the rest is self-taught and that is very commendable. He holds all the towns meetings, speaks at these woman's conventions and several leading functions. I think he spoke at the Red Hat Society our ladies had here a couple of weeks ago, I ain't sure about that. We are right proud of him even though some of us are outcast, he sure is a single flower in a field of weeds; now we have to be careful cause as we college people say, he hasn't come out of the barn yet.

When he does he will probably want to join the <u>United States Militia</u> and go overseas. Maybe Bill Clinton will help him, maybe he has already, I don't know for sure. Aw Rafe ain't you sumpen!

Our area resident's work very hard to keep up their district, they will put in all day some Saturdays to rework the town flower garden. Some of the prior town politics have built a town park and the girls nearly kill themselves making it pretty. I think Rose Jean put some tulips their, Ella Ruby made ribbon for the benches and ole Bubba Joe built all the benches a flower trellis and what ever you call those round things or octagon. Billy Bob brought Hoover his English pit bull to keep watch over it and make sure nobody stole anything.

Now, another problem has arisen from enlisting Hoover, we don't know who is going to clean up after him. Poor Hoover is nearing twenty and don't get around well and I worry about him being able to protect it sufficiently. Billy Bob says, "if Hoover does get a hold on them they won't get away." Hoover weighs in at about one hundred thirty and his back legs are stiff with arthritis.

We are trying to build our town up to attract more residents and businesses. Our mayor is really working hard on it and he doesn't go along with some of the prior mayors, he doesn't want to make our town a retirement town. The most powerful statement I ever heard Billy Bob make was, " Once we get all the water and sewer lines repaired and get this town smelling better I am going to start putting some of that tax money around the outer limits of our town and make it beautiful, so people will want to start moving here." That Billy Bob is a sure enuff Politician, some of the bigger farmers follow him around like Hoover, of course Hoover is first.

We have a railroad track that comes through town close to where the supermarket use to be and I wouldn't be surprised to hear Billy Bob say that he was going to try and get it moved. It is an eye sore for the town and it ain't any use in it, it never stops to unload anything until it gets way north of town. It also is a hindrance to Billy Bob's son Trace Richard Yoder, from his first marriage. Billy Bob's first wife was a Mennonite. When Trace comes through town on Saturday night in his four-wheel drive Dodge, you know the one with the six little headlights.

Poor Trace has to slow down to fifty miles an hour to get across the tracks without turning over his beauty. First green and pink John Deere four wheel drive Dodge I have ever seen, I think. He would be heart broken if he were to wreck that truck. Trace doesn't have a girlfriend yet, he said there weren't any girls in this town pretty enough to ride in his truck. Sounds like he is really proud of his truck and besides Billy Bob told him if he broke this one he could walk.

Our town got a grant this year to tear down three houses and build new ones to replace them. I sure am glad that FEMA wasn't in charge of replacing them with all them leftover trailers from hurricane Katrina. I guess you know what the people would wind up living in if that were the case. I hear next year the farmers may get a grant to replace thirty-five pig parlors and six feeder houses.

I reckon all in all we are doing pretty good, the town collected five thousand eighty-two dollars last year in taxes. We got a new pizza parlor first of the month and they are raking in four or five customers every day and that means more taxes. We still have a bank, a school up through the eighth grade, a city hall, a shoe repair shop, flower shop and a big hardware store. We have been lucky so far Wila-Mart shopping center has only closed our super market, Ben Franklins, two hair-fixing shops and two gas stations. Those two gas stations were good ones too, the kind where some one pumps gas for you, washes your winshield and takes your money, full service I believe they call it, I'm not sure. We sure do miss them anyway, says Beal Poyter a drifter.

Now the reason we call Beal a drifter is because every summer Beal drifts off up to Alaska in search of gold. I ask Beal last year if I could go with him that I might bring good luck to him.

Somehow I got the impression that he didn't want me to go, cause he said, Nah you wouldn't like the climate. You wouldn't fit in too good up their anyway you just being a hillbilly and all. Well I knew he was afraid he might strike gold this year and if I was along I would know where his strike was located. I guess he is afraid I might come back and tell his brother-in-law James R. Grinning about it. I don't know if James would want a slice of the pie or not.

Oh I almost forgot, we do have a conveince store and they do sell gas, but won't pump it. All they seem to be interested in is taking your money, convience? They do sell beer and lottery tickets just in case some poor sole is a little tanked up and happens to have a few extra dollars left on him. The state sure is hanging in there to get their share of our children's supper. Dr. Lila Emma Ruth hangs out there a lot, maybe she thinks some poor soul might come in all down and out and need her. That way she would be right handy and be able to help them right away, Now that's a real Dr. for you, give up her time for the needy. Now I am not sure, but I think I heard that the Little Gargoyle convenience store is renting her a room to practice her medicine in.

I went to our local medical center today where they were having an open house to try to interest more people to come there for their medical needs. Our local Dr. is not really a Doctor he is just a nurse practicioner, but he can doctor you better than a lot of these died in the wool doctors. We have a man in an adjoining town that is supposed to be a doctor that most folks wouldn't use as a veternarian. You know I can't blame them, I guess. It is a shame that we have people with degrees whom are allowed to practice a professional trade who need to go back through grade school and the works. My friend Bubba says, a child could do as well as some of them, and with a lot more common sense.

P.S. Love your enemy and drive'm nuts!

CHAPTER THREE
Our Farmers

Now everybody the world over knows that our farmers feed the world. It is a great responsibility, but somebody's got to do it. Cause I read once and heard Rafe say in one of his speeches that countries like France, Germany, Italy, Austria and a few others do not have enough arable land to raise their food. Mighty big places not to be able to raise their own food, but I guess it would be sort of hard to raise corn and soybeans on a mountainside or in a desert. No matter, but what the heck is an arable land pray tell?

I also heard that these countries are forgetting who is raising their grub, and are coming over here where it is provided and raising all kinds of hell. I read something one fella wrote that said they could go home if they don't like us. Why did they come over here in the first place if they didn't like us. Planning on taking over maybe, maybe I'm wrong. Fella is what the socially correct are calling Southerners now maybe even Yankees too, I think.

Our farmers use to work their fingers to the bone as the old saying goes. Their crops were a gamble every year if I may use the term. Bubba Joe was an ole time farmer, he never had a whole lot of money left over after paying the bank back what they loaned him in the spring. Bubba Joe would get up in the morning, put on his knee boots and go to the barn. After feeding the hogs and cows he would come back to the house to change shoes, cause he couldn't afford but one pair of them expensive knee boots a year. He would stop outside and rinse his boots off before going into the utility room to change.

That room smelled just like pig poop and his wife Helen Sue would yell at him about stinking up the house. I washed my boots outside was his argument. Yes you did but you did not wash Bubba, you are going to smell like pig manure all day. I declare Bubba Joe you smell like a barnyard all the time, I sure wish I had known this before we married. Bubba Joe was about to come to the conclusion that Helen Sue didn't love him any more until their first child came along after being married for seven years.

"Bubba Joe you are wonderful, she said, and now I am going to have a little Bubba Joe." Bubba asked her what she was going to name the baby and she said, "Bubba Joe Junior, if it's a boy and Bubba Jean if it's a girl." "You can't name her Bubba, Helen."

"I ain't goin to name her Bubba Helen, I said Bubba Jean." "But you can't" he said. "If you think I can't just watch me Buster."

"My name is Bubba."

Anyway Bubba and Helen have three boys now and they are crazy about each other. Bubba said he sure did enjoy watching little Bubba 1, Bubba 2 and Bubba 3 playing in the yard, and under Helens watchful eye Bubba 1 is always the leader.

Billy Bob gets one of them farm magazines once a month still. He used to be the biggest farmer around these parts, but he sold out a few years ago because his first wife ran off with a local carpenter. Billy Bob thought the carpenter was taking a long time repairing the porch, but Billy Bob wouldn't bring it up to his wife.

Then one day a month later soon after the carpenter finished with the porch they both came up missing.

Some of the locals never figured it out, but Billy Bob did. He soon just sold out and left the farm couldn't keep his mind on his business, said he would get into Politics he might be able to make it there. Besides his three old cows had lost so much weight he knew he couldn't make a profit from them.

Soon after Billy Bob got into politics he came into a pile of money from somewhere, probably inherited it don't you think? I was surprised that he bought his sixty acres back and another forty from a man named George Washington who wanted to move back to New England. I have often wondered where that is. I don't believe I have ever heard of a state with that name, sounds sort of fishy to me. I don't know how, but Billy Bob is one of our richest residents now. Everybody looks up to him as a natural born leader and politician!

Rafe don't do much of anything that I know of except sit around the country under windows with that danged guitar of his.

They say he is a pretty good singer, but I ain't never heard him so I couldn't say. I did hear him yell once when a group of young pranksters threw a firecracker under his chair when he was dating Rose Jean. I heard them telling later that Rafe was right up in Rose Jean's face jest about to kiss her when the firecracker went off and Rafe stuck his tongue up her nose. They said he spit and sputtered so much it made Rose Jean so mad at him she wouldn't talk to him for several weeks.

I don't really understand why farmers are so in love with the land and the hard work of raising row crops to feed so many people. Calculating in accordance with the textbooks, television and computers there are nigh onto five billion people that we are feeding from our croplands. Did you know to give everyone a single roasted ear of corn, it would take all the corn grown in Illinois, Indiana and Iowa. That is a lot of corn just for a small portion of one meal. I don't know about the Orient, do Japanese eat corn? Do Japanese horses eat corn too? Even after being to college there is still so terribly much I don't know!

Fertilizer was bad enough it took about five years for our farmers to get use to using the stuff. This was nothing however compared to weed and pest control. The names alone was enough to keep our farmers batty forever. Poor fellows have been going to schools, seminars and buying books and magazines by the pound. Just anything that had the words pest or weed control, but it hasn't really helped that much.

Bubba Joe said he had learned enough to know which to put in the barn and which to put in the field. Our mayor told him that they both went in the field and Bubba responded with, "see there them durned government boys are lying to us again. They are afraid we are going to make a little money and they ain't gonna be able to get their fingers in it."

Bubba did admit though that it was pretty good stuff to have around. He claims it keeps the weeds out of his garden all year long and he hasn't had to hoe it one time yet.

He also believes it to be pretty good medicine when you need it. According to Bubba Joe he had a biggg Knot to come up on his arm a few days ago. In spite of everything he did it would not go away. Then four days later he was putting some pesticide on his crop and spilled a little on his arm and mysteriously it just went away. We never know what just might turn up later as medicine. One farmer claims his cows had the hollow tail! When they git it he says, they loose their appetite and come to the barn. It has even cost me some calves he raved on.

I figgered it out though said he, and what to do about it. He claimed, that you had to slit there tail and fill it with a paste made from mustard and red pepper, bandage them and turn'em loose. The farmer didn't mention it , but you had better be out of their way, too. He declared it would make them well again. He said, they would go back out to the pasture almost immediately, but then I probably would, too. The ole farmer vowed that the only adverse effect it had on them was that it tore their bowels up a little, can't you imagine?

There are getting to be more horses kept on farms again and a lot of people who aren't farmers are keeping horses. Horses need corn and we gotta grow it, do horses eat the cob, too? Horses probably eat three ears of corn a meal, so if there are only one billion horses in the world there goes another three billion ears and another six states. Feeding stock can be very expensive at times, I mean five billion humans fed one meal and one billion horses fed one meal using up nine states is hard on our corn yield for a year. Why there would hardly be enough left for Japan and Holland. I can see where grass comes in so important now.

I did the math for a year against the above statistics and just to give everyone one ear a meal a week times four weeks a month is two hundred fifty billion ears a year. I couldn't even guess how many states it would take to supply that much corn.

Then one billion horses at three meals a day and three ears per meal, astronomical. Now try matching those statistics to soybeans. Sure is a good thing that horses will eat carrots, too. Of course, hay and grass helps out as well.

We have a farmer in the community who seems to really get carried away about his crop yield. I have never figured out why, but it always appears to be mostly about his corn crop. One year the others put together a scheme to see just how far he would go and that year he made one hundred fifty barrels of corn per acre.

The largest yield ever recorded till that day was forty barrel.

Bubba Joe and Billy Bob had a relative in Chicago who came visiting last year. Tom Bill Jiskin was a younger man than his relatives, but appeared to know about everything, so they decided to put one over on him one morning. They took him to breakfast at the Snack Shop and as they were having sausage, eggs and coffee they heard a plane going over. Billy Bob reached over with his foot and mashed Bubba's toe and said. "Bubba you hear that plane?" Bubba said, "yeah why,"

"Sounds like he is having trouble to me, what do you think?"

"Could be the way it sounds, what do you think, Tom Bill?"

Tom Bill said, "Yeah, outside engine on the right is missing a little."

Needless to say they didn't try pulling anything else on Tom Bill. Funny thing was after he went back to Chicago they found out that he had worked on airplanes engines for five years and they still don't know if Tom knew what he was taking about or not!

Farmers are a bunch of good ole boys with a sense of humor and were the ones who invented the bartering system. Bobby Joe Harris was one of those type people and would walk ten miles to get to help another farmer in need, especially if he had a good looking daughter. One of the older farmers had a barn to blow down in a storm and put out the word. Just so happen this farmer had a young son who had not gotten all his masculine features yet,

So for a prank he dressed his young son up as a girl and waited for Bobby Joe to show up. It was told later that Bobby Joe followed his son around all day and didn't do hardly any work at all. At the end of the day the farmer took the girls clothes off his son. It kind of hurt Bobby Joes feelings a little he said, that he knew it wasn't a girl all day, that she didn't smell just right to be a girl.

I tell you though, we got to be proud of our farmers they are very important. All the crops they raise has kept the world fed both human and domestic animals. I have thought about it a lot and have come to the conclusions that if it weren't for them we might have wound up like the King in the Bible whom God put out in the field grazing with the animals. If that were the case you know we might have never invented the bathroom.

We got a piece of land in our county about fifteen hundred acres large that is right on the edge of the swamp. At certain times of the year when there is lots of rain, water almost completely encircles the piece of land and I guess that is why they named it Beech Ridge. The ridge has approximately fifteen hundred acres of the finest land in the county. A few years back about ten different families lived on the ridge, farmed and survived.

After a few years of living their and farming the people began to slowly move away from the ridge. It is still farmed and fondly remembered as a brooding ground, a farming ground, a fishing and hunting ground and a place to get away from. But I guess what it is most remembered for is its production of cottonmouth or water moccasins, and a mosquito or two.

Us young boys use to go to beech ridge and shoot the cottonmouths on Sunday afternoon. We would shoot snakes all afternoon and never miss a shot and never miss a snake. When we would shoot one, another would take its place. When it grew close to night we would leave as not to get bitten and the limbs would be laying just as full as when we came. We didn't know the danger we were in and if God hadn't went with us I wouldn't be writing this today.

Some Southern story tellers even claim to have spent the afternoon on the lake shooting mosquitoes. I haven't personally seen any mosquitoes that big, but I can't call them liars. Bubba Joe says that hidden in them cypress knees are mosquitoes as big as sparrows.

We were told that if we would wear hip boots the snakes wouldn't bite us that they couldn't bite through rubber boots.

However I finally figured out that hip boots didn't come up but so high. They didn't cover anything above the waist and some of the most important things I got is above the waist.

Since I don't have a brain I don't have to worry about that, but my mouth is above my waist and I have to eat. My stomach is above my waist and I do have to process what I eat so I can eat some more. My breast are above my waist so my wife can kiss them and say, gotcha. My ears are above my waist so I can hear her say, gotcha. My nose is above my waist so I can keep my head cleared out just in case I should get a brain. So you see above the waist is very important.

Well a long time ago the children ran rampant over Beech Ridge. Their little squeals of happeness was heard from one end of the ridge to the other. When they becames teenagers the boys cussin was heard all over the ridge and the girls little squeals of pleasure as well. Dogs barked continuously as the chased the children, the cats meowed, the birds chirped, the ground hogs ran away fearfully and the snails just jaunted along unaware.

When the boys taught the girls how to kiss, you talk about chirping!!! Beech Ridge was a wonderful place to grow up, I guess it was a whole lot like King Edward Island, just a good place to be.

Now there were the Burpoles who lived on Beech Ridge and came to America from Salzburg, Austria. They forgot what their name was in Austria so they just chose Burpole. Tom Burpole was the fathers name, Evelyn was the mother and two daughters Janet and Julie. Most everbody laughed at their last name, but personally I didn't think they did any better on the first names. I believe I could have done much better on their first names like Tommy Jack Burpole and Evelyn Joyce Burpole, and for the girls they could have been something more civil like Janet Pearl and Julie Ruth Burpole, much better don't you think?

Well the ridge turned out a lot of fine specimens in those days and they all grew up to be something great. There was Bobby Gene Mackin who became a brain surgeon and teaches at some big hospital in Nashville. He teaches how to remove the hemotobin or something from the brain while operating. Janet and Julie are both nurses and good ones they say. One of them nurses people and the other nurses animals.

Then there was the Abernathy twins who both turned out to be schoolteachers. Susan R. Beebers who made a doctor, Jerlean Biswack is in social working, Eugene Cartwright is a welder and finally the little girl everyone called Sherbert made a doctor too, but I don't know what kind of work she does, Dr. assistant maybe.

People around here still reminiss about the mules they use to work on the ridge, the big watermelons they use to grow and who caught the biggest fish on Sunday afternoon. A fight between eighty year olds is not unheard of in those discussions, but most of them take all evening. Those were the days!

P.S. Do you know the quickest way to tame the Iraquis? Put them in overalls, behind a team of mules and teach the how to raise cotton.

CHAPTER FOUR
Town Meetings

Our town has a meeting of the minds every first Tuesday of the month, here they will discuss any old business that was not taken care of at the last meeting. Of course that doesn't take very long. the meeting of the minds leastwise. Then they introduce any new business that has come up since, but that's where it stops being anywhere near the same as any other meeting in the world.

Guess I shouldn't laugh at them they do pretty good for what they have to work with. They don't really hurt each other though sometimes you think they are going to. They have gone far enough to have a snowball battle one winter and broke Rose Jeans glasses. The town had to reimburse her for her glasses and Billy Bob, he's the town mayor, griped about that for a year.

Of course Billy Bob, the mayor, opens the meeting and turns it over to a chairperson, which I don't understand. For as I know they all sit in chairs, may be some secret code, I could be wrong. The chairperson initiates a business subject before the board members and from their on its open house. it's a knock down, drag out, cat scratch dog fight the rest of the night.

You will usually see them start coming out about nine-thirty all red in the face, jaws pooched out just like they were raving mad. All except for Billy Bob who always has a smile on his face like he had just won a battle. Rose Jean said at the last meeting she never heard such foul things come out of the mouths of good Christian people in her life.

They approved an order at one meeting that all dogs running free were to be shot. Billy Bob jumped all over that with both barrels open, he didn't want Hoover shot. So Billy Bob told them that Hoover had the job of guarding the town park and was an employee of the town. When pressed harder about the subject he produced paperwork showing where he had paid Hoover one hundred dollars a week for the past ten months. Hoover was then relished by the towns people for taking very good care of the town park.

Billy Bob (our mayor) has an impeccable inner statute. He will tell you that he does not believe in the fleecing of others or of a town. That all things should be kept conscionable and completely on the level. That all records should be kept where they will withstand severe scrutiny. What a great man?

One of his friends told him that he should let the town pay for his fuel and insurance on his car since he drove it on town business. Billy Bob laughed and reported to his friend, :you know me better than that Carl." Write that down Lila Mae, we may need it to help us recognize some jackleg trying to take the town for a few bucks." Turning back to his friend he said, " if there is anything I hate Carl, its some sneaky little snot nose trying to take advantage of innocent people."

Our mayor Billy Bob loves education, he uses the town tax base to help education as often as he can. Just last month the school was putting on a play outside the school building. Food vendors were invited to come set up their equipment to sell sandwiches. Most of them try to donate seventy-five per-cent of their profit. This leaves twenty-five peer-cent to pay for the transporting and setting up the equipment.

Billy Bob brought his vending equipment early and set up nearest the stage. When it was over he donated twenty-five per-cent of his profits. When Bubba ask him why he did not donate the usual, he told Bubba that the expenses were going up everyday and that they had become astronomical. Every one thought Billy Bob had gotten mad and started cussing so they didn't push it any further.

Billy Bob has a girl friend he goes around with, maybe two, I am not sure but he calls her his private secretary. There must be something to it because they are always in private when she secs. I guess that is what a secretary does, I could be wrong. She goes everywhere Billy Bob goes and stays until they get done. She has always got a briefcase and an overnight bag so I am sure they are carrying town records and such.

Funny thing happened to Billy Bob once. He and his private secretary were going on a trip to take care of some very important town business. They got there late so they had to check into a hotel room until the next morning. Billy Bob was taking off his pants when he heard a police siren go off outside the building so he takes off hoping over to the window to see what his next move should be. Sadly he stumbled and fell right through the hotel window, all the way to a group of flowered bushes below. On the way down his pants got caught on a window hook and yanked them right off his carcass. As far as we know they are still hanging there. We have heard that the hotel uses it as advertising and business has picked up by fifty per-cent.

The town has put women in most of the town seat positions and you talk about hilarious. Most have never taken care of any business of that sort, some has never handled any business and the rest don't know what it means. Wish I had a disc copy of one of their meetings I could be a rich man. If Hollywood could sit in on one of those meetings we would be on the map.

I haven't figured out why Bill Bob has quit trying to entice new business into our town. He knows more business brings in more taxes, but he may have all the money he wants or is afraid he can't handle a larger tax base.

The town has a couple of old buildings he is trying to find a use for, that will cost almost as much to repair and maintain as it would to build a new one. He claims to be intending to put a museum in one of them. Someone ask him, a museum for what, to show off old buildings. We surely don't have any resources that we could use for a museum display. There may be more money in the museum business than we think for, I don't know.

The city board has been having meetings on these new subjects, but no one will talk about them. I guessed that maybe they were ashamed to bring them up, but I guess maybe I had better not be to hasty, Billy Bob has pulled a rabbit out of his hat more than once. You never can tell about our mayor he can at times be a real magician, I think that is what you call it, I'm not sure.

He drove his old farm truck down the road by the mental establishment in our county one-day and his right back wheel came off and rolled past him up the road. He got out of the truck and retrieved his wheel and jacked up the truck. He walked around the truck a few times and slapped his leg with a loud curse he determined that he had lost all the lug nuts for that wheel. How in the world am I going to get this truck home he pondered. After an hour of hard concentration a young man inside the fence of the sanitarium called to him and informed him he could take one nut from each other wheel which would give him three lug nuts for his crippled wheel, that should get you home.

Billy Bob was dumbfounded and asked the young man, "man what are you doing in that place with such mentality?" Well I may be crazy, but I'm not stupid ," the young man replied. Billy Bob was so shook up he went all over town repeating the story.

P.S. You want to elect a President that really knows how to run America? Elect one out of Billy Bob University!

CHAPTER FIVE
Town Businesses

It is hard to keep up with our town businesses there are a few left and a few gone. It appears the list is changing almost every day. At the last count we had seventeen businesses in town, but no supermarket. We have approximately one thousand residents and no way to feed them. Every town around us does have a supermarket and three to five grocery stores of some kind even if they are all called convenience stores. Well we have a convenience store and two restaurants. So if you've got money you can eat and not have to cook, that will please the ladies. See the benefits of having ladies on the city board.

Bubba's wife came to him a couple of weeks ago bringing up the subject of vacation. She told him that he had worked hard this spring and had earned a vacation. It's a good idea he told here, now where would you like to go, back to Branson Missouri. I don't think so, she exhaled we been there too many times. I think I would like to go someplace I don't go very often. So Bubba suggested the kitchen, but he didn't suggest the skinned place above his right ear. He also earned the right to sleep on the couch for a week.

Most of our town businesses don't spend any money so they don't make any money. Rafe held a business meeting when he first moved to town about not writing sales receipt and not putting any money in the bank. Your Uncle Sam will not be able to trace it that way, he explained. He proposed that it would make good camping trip money and fishing money. He also stressed to them that above all they were not to cheat.

Car sales are going good this year. Our local car dealership is selling a car a month and fixing up two. Our garage is fixing up the two cars a month for the dealer. Billy Bob and the bank are loaning money to those who buy locally.

Our mayor Billy Bob is always happy to pick up second mortgages on houses and property locally. It appears that the towns people are clinging to Billy Bob's last directive about keeping our money in town. Keep your money in town folks, don't let these other towns in on any of our hard earned money. That way we can just circulate it and there will always be money for our town to live off of. I declare sometimes he sounds just like the CEO of an insurance company.

The bank has just learned the power of advertising and the power of women. Last week they started giving free hair styling with every new loan and a free meal for every monthly payment made. An new man in town came in last week wanting the bank to finance a rutabaga farm and the bank wouldn't touch it. Billy Bob was a bit reluctant , but finally gave in at twenty-six per-cent interest on the money. Billy is helping out the community every chance he gets, I think.

If everything goes right in another twenty years Billy Bob will own everything in a hundred mile radius. The only way Billy Bob will ever know what the word radius means, is if it is explained to him in terms of recycling his money.

The town City Hall is very active this year making new plans, beefing up old ones and finding new women to fill certain positions. We now boast a mayor, city manager who has just been promoted from city recorder and I am not sure, she may just fill both positions. We have a city clerk who is doing her work and the city recorders work and over half of the city managers. I don't know how she manages to do so much work. I am not sure, but I think she is putting in sixty hours work and getting paid for thirty and even that is cut rate.

We also have three under paid maintenance men and eight city cops. I ain't never figured out why so many cops, when they all come to town it looks like a coyote pack in uniform. We have no crime and the mayor claims it is because we have enough cops to scare them off.

When someone gets stopped for doing thirty in a thirty mile an hour speed zone there are usually three cop cars on the scene. I guess they are afraid poor ole ninety three year old Marvin has a truckload of dope he is trying to sell. Either that or has a couple of bombs he is trying to sneak downtown and blow up the town he has lived in all his life. Marvin is a threat to society, but those teens running around armed to the hilt is no threat. Make a mayor get on Prozac, don't you think?

One cop was checking out an old building he heard they were making meth in. He sneaked up the side of the building, stumbled on a rock and shot himself in the arm. Poor fella, injured on duty. Another cop I hear takes his target practice just outside the city limits sign

I heard, don't know how true it is, that the mayor gave his city manager an astronomical raise, second raise she got in two days. I heard she got a two-dollar at one time, the maintenance supervisor that has been with the city for nearly twenty-five years got less than a dollar and the clerk who does about all the office work got nothing, fair. Billy Bob of course is not going to tell that he will be too busy telling everyone to be a good and decent Christian. A friend of mine said, that there was more butter in the dish than it looked like it was. There just may be more in the dish than just butter.

We have three maintenance men who relish getting on the site when a call is made and repairing it right the first time. Billy Bob is unrelenting at times about him being the engineer on certain jobs. These are usually the kind of jobs where the routing and cost will be a little higher. I seen one of these jobs where a frozen water line was being repaired in the towns Library. Billy Bob had the line routed inside the building along the floor and wall very visible to the naked eye. He maintained that the water line would not freeze on the inside and he does have a point there, wouldn't you think?

Billy Bob's city manager has been making his mayor meetings for him and no one can figure out why! Perhaps she is planning on being the next mayor or maybe just taking a day to play. There is a lot of murmuring over town about this girl. Some say she is meeting friends and some think she has been working with the bigger town's TV station trying to get on one of those makeover shows. Some say she needs it and others don't think it will do much good. I would be ashamed to say such a thing about the poor lady, she has enough problems.

She is not really ugly like the locals are suggesting, but I would vote for the makeover. She bought her a pug bulldog once so she would have someone to take with her that looked worse than she did when she went shopping. She once got a contract for one of these soap commercials, but they chose her sight unseen. Well a few days later they got her picture in the mail so they could setup some commercial scenes. She never told us why they used the loggerhead turtle in the scenes instead of her. I sure hate to talk about the poor girl, but the loggerhead was an improvement.

The other office girl, now here is a nice looking woman and very intelligent too. She sure outshines her boss by a country mile. When Betty Faye Minswaulk gets tired from doing all the work she hands the city managers picture on the office door and no one will come in as long as its there. It is the only way the poor girl can get to take a break!

The city barbershop and two hairdressers count as one business. They all three get seventeen customers a week and that is not each.

One of the hairdressers is still using hairstyles from 1965 or earlier. This week her rival ran a promo on permanents from 1948 and they didn't look too very bad, just stood a little too high on the head. At least they are trying, I think.

The barbershop is still cutting a little close on the bottom, looks like a freshly peeled apple around the neck and ears. Looks like the barber could get away from these old style haircuts. He probably knows about the newer styles, I am not sure.

He also offers a full line of earrings for his more feminine clientele. He sold a world of those things to until he went up to seventy-five cents a pair. It sure looked a mess around here for a while. Billy Bob claimed it was ok for men to wear earrings if they wanted to, I know Billy Bob he wouldn't have said such a thing if he hadn't financed the purchased of those things. He was also instrumental in getting toe rings in town for women and…..guys. Could you men imagine trading your brogans for sandals and toe rings? Don't it make you just want to moon walk?

So far Rafe is the only questionable one we got, he bought some toe rings and earrings. He claims that more educated people wear them and can't figure out why the three college grads ain't got some of them, duhhh. We got two men standing behind the barn door with two by fours with nails drove through them just waiting for him to come through the barn door or whatever you call it.

We have a lot of good businessmen down South. Most people don't seem to realize just how good our business minds are in the South. I always figured anyone who could take a bunch of old wrecked cars and make a living out of them was either extremely lucky or a great business mind.

Then there are the car lots having cars priced $500.00 or below, selling enough of them to build a new house must also be a good business mind. Then there are the miracle workers who own an old ton and a half flat bed truck buying other peoples junk at $5.00 a load and living off of it is a very slick businessperson. The ones who really surprised me were the women who used other peoples merchandise, having parties at other peoples houses and actually selling it to everyone woman in town are some pretty slick operators.

Alford Joe figures him out a plan to do just that and make a lot of money for both him and the surrounding farmers, but he couldn't talk the farmers to let him have the hogs on consignment.

I was once told that business people in the South had to be above average business people just to maintain their business, great business managers to make their businesses rate in the top ten of the South. Mediocre managers here usually last a couple of years and then out. In an article I read once a couple of years back the writer advocated that two years was pretty much the trial period

For a new business. That if they were not making money by then, there was no rhyme or reason to go any further.

Our mayor Billy Bob is considered a good business mind, because he took the beginning tax income of eight thousand five hundred dollars and ran a town of 1200 people. Of course the bank helped out a lot, but that was not the deciding factor. What really stood out was the fact that Billy Bob paid himself $20,000.00 the first year and his pit bull got $5,200.00 for his first years work.

Then the mayor really surprised the town by initiating two new programs at the tune of $5,000.00 each a year. That is doing pretty good on an $8,5000.00 tax base. It does look like Billy Bob could have won some kind of plaque for his efforts. It was told that the state thought there was some under handed dealing going on somewhere, however they couldn't find the first thing.

I couldn't believe that they would think such a thing about our mayor. I thought they were probably just jealous or just didn't know how to be frugal.

Frugal is Billy Bob's middle name even when it comes to Trace Richard. Billy Bob loves to make money, but he hates to spend it worse than any man I have ever seen. In his world spending is a no-no. He will hardly eat because he has to pay for it, isn't that be a little to tight? When he is invited to one of our town functions that includes potluck dinners or any kind of a free meal he sure can put it away. If it weren't for free meals our mayor probably wouldn't be here for us to brag on. He is just skin and bones, poor fellow.

I guess the most he has ever spent at one time, was on Trace Richard after Trace had experienced a long sickness. The mayor bought Trace a Harley spending almost ten thousand on it and accessories. Later Billy Bob cried like a baby. I have never seen anything like it, he sat in his big office chair and wet eight big hankerchiefs.

Trace really disappointed his Father. Billy Bob said; " he looks awful, my son is a hippie and he smells bad, after all I have done for him he smells". Trace did look terrible, he had grown him long hair and a beard, he plaited his hair and let it fall down his back in a pigtail and it swung from side to side when he walked. Trace looked like he hadn't seen any water since he and his friends camped out on the Mississippi river a couple of years back. Billy Bob said; "he looks just like some of them dirty ole mechanics I seen in Louisiana that worked on the boat docks.

Finally five years later Billy Bob shamed Trace into cleaning up and he immediately became a happier man. It got rid of the dark spots under Billy Bob's eyes and he began to look a lot better. I really felt better for the mayor, it added ten years to his looks.

P.S. Want to know how to get American labor back on the right track? Take the Federal Bank away from the British!

CHAPTER SIX
Our School

Yeah, we still got one up to the ninth grade and still kinda proud of it too. We had a high until 1982 when the county high and mighties claimed we needed to offer more than just reeden, <u>ridin</u> and rithmetic so they sent them off to the next town. We wanted to keep our high school, but I guess we can't have everything.

We sent our children on to another town that look down there noses at us because we were a small town high school. We got placed at the back of the classrooms and wondered if the grades we got were accurate. The snickering behind their hands made us feel like we had come up out of the woods to go to school. Ole Billy Bob cautioned everyone not to say anything about it and it would all pass and for once he was right about a school matter.

Billy Bob is not always right about matters pertaining to the school system, he realized that and you guessed it, he put a woman in charge of school curriculums. He is putting women in charge of nearly everything. Our mayor sure has a thing about women and I hear he likes to sit in their lap too I hear, but I could be wrong. He informs city workers if they have a complaint about any of the women in his government to come to him with it and he will get it straight with them and I'd bet on that.

We had a principle a while back that gave a spanking to a fourteen-year-old girl. He got carried away with the job and left some marks on one of her legs. It of course upset the family to no end and they set out to get him relieved of his position. While investigating the complaint they found out that he had a few days before taken two teens cell phones. After keeping them for a couple of days her called the girls in and offered to give back the phones if they would give him a kiss. And I suppose that meant a kiss from each of them, don't you think? Well this got him in a little deeper than ever, but Ole Billy Bob kind of stood up for him.

He said that the principle made a mistake for sure, that he should have had a woman to spank her instead.

It kind of makes you wonder about the two of them, due to the principles actions and then our mayors reactions it appears they might have been a little bit kin. Well as usual the principle got away with it except he can't teach in our county any longer and Billy Bob was relieved. I am not sure about it, but I wouldn't be surprised if he went to an adjoining county and spanked him another teenager. He needs to have to go back to school on properly executing principle ship. You know the old saying though, you can lead a mule to water, but you can't make him drink.

These new schools they are building are far better than the old ones, because they are bigger and cost more. The rooms are larger and you can get more children in each classroom cutting back on teachers. This saves more money to be used in other areas, such as teachers aides, where the teacher has more time to go to the office and hang out with the principle. That's important you know we need more teacher and principle bonding. The child's education may be suffering a little, but you can't have everything. Besides the parents should be teaching them more at home.

Some of that money saved can be used on summer school for pre-kindergarten children. They take them to summer schools and teach them to write their name and draw pictures. The lazy parents have not already taught them to draw pictures after work. These Moms are so lazy all they have to do after getting up at four o'clock and getting things ready so there children are properly dressed for school, getting herself ready for work, putting in a days work, picking her children up at the sitter's house, coming home and making supper, washing clothes, washing dishes, cleaning up the kitchen, helping the children with homework, making sure Tommy doesn't hang the dog, bringing daddy a sandwich and a beer to the couch or his easy chair, picking up the clothes daddy left in the bathroom floor, lowering the commode seat ten times that the males of the house left up, putting the kids to bed on time so they get ample rest and brings daddy another beer. Then she can sit down and rest until bedtime, a whole fifteen minutes. Of course they then must go to bed because daddy needs her again. Yeah buddy, they are the weaker sex. By that time, after that amount of work if they are not weak then they are not human.

Bubba Joe's wife says that is why women cry so much. They have to have an avenue of relief from somewhere. She said Bubba Joe thought he was the one responsible for that, silly man. Bubba Joe is a big man with wide shoulders and a very masculine mentality I can see where he would think that, silly man.

When Billy Bob was married to his first wife they went in the bedroom one night to go to bed and Billy Bob said, " Martha I am going to make you the happiest woman in the world tonight." And Martha just smiled and promptly responded, "I'm a gonna miss you Billy Bob." Poor Billy Bob was quite then and didn't say nothing the rest of the night.

Did you hear the bell ring Martha Ann? I sure did guess its time to get back to school? What do you think?

When we still had our high school Bubba went through the tenth grade there. As a mater of fact Bubba only went through the tenth grade, said he didn't need to be a graduate to milk cows and slop the hogs. Anyway on his first day in the tenth grade his teacher told him that they were going to be studying music. So the following day Bubba brought his guitar with him and set out to give them lessons. That Bubba now he is one more guitar picker, when he plays wildwood flower, it'll make your skin crawl.

One Sunday afternoon Bubba had a whole yard full of visitors at his house and he was entertaining them. He played and sang the song, "if I could hear my mother pray again" when he finished singing there was not a dry eye in the crowd. Everyone told the reason they were crying was because Bubba was so passionate about the loss of his mother. I got kinda tickled because Bubba's mother lives in Arkansas.

Bubba's best friend Alford Joe Horner didn't get his homework one afternoon for helping his father in the field. The next morning when he got up he ask his mother if he could just stay home because he didn't have his lessons. I guess so she told Alford go on to the field and help Papa. When Alford did go back his teacher ask him why he wasn't at school yesterday. He told the teacher it was because he didn't have his lessons. Why Alford I ought to give you a whipping for missing school over something like that. Afraid he was going to get a spanking Alford to the teacher that it was his mother's fault. You expect me to believe that? Well I ask her if I could stay home and she said she guessed so, that she wouldn't want to hear the old bat rave all day for nothing, either. Mrs. Peckinpaugh was actually real sweet to him the rest of the day.

Our school days were something to remember, some of the best days of our life, we just didn't know it then. In most of the classes at Richwood School it was pretty well evened out with boys and girls. We chased the girls and they ran and screamed as if they were dying, it was the only way they could get us to chase them. Sometimes we caught'em sometimes we didn't. I have often wondered if they wanted us to catch'em or not, they sure acted like they didn't.

Martha Ann and Mavis Anne were me and Bubba's girlfriends. They got to be our girlfriends when we started chasing them and when we caught'em bingo they were our girlfriends. I was always more careful who I chased when I got older. A man could get into a lifetime of trouble like that. Bubba got to be more cautious too especially after we had to sit under a tarpaulin with them one afternoon when it rained. I got afraid for Bubba that day, why Mavis was making all kind of smacking noises on Bubba's neck, giggling and squealing like a pig under a fence. She went wheeee Oh Bubba. You never seen anybody run as fast as Bubba did when he finally did get away from Mavis Anne. Mavis cried and ran after Bubba for a week.

Bubba Joe and I learned a lot about life at that little school and I think we both realized later that we could have had a whole lot more fun.

Richwood School had a creek that ran behind the school that the river ran into a few miles up the road. Bubba Joe and Alford Joe kept some fishing poles hid along the bank for emergency purposes. Every now and then they would skip and hour of classes and go fishing. One day they came in from their fishing excursion with gook all over their hands where they had been taking the fish off the hooks. Alford grabbed Mavis Anne's skirt and got some fish on her. As a result Alford got expelled from school for three days and poor Mavis had to go home with a note from her teacher.

We never forgot our school days and at occasions we like to get together and remember the good ole days.

P.S. We could get our schools and Universities leveled out and productive again if we would let the children teach for a couple years, with the exception of Berkley. They're probably more intelligent!

CHAPTER SEVEN
Livelihoods

Now we are all grown up and are in the real world and as Bubba says, what a change. We came to know more about girls and now we both have families. I got a boy and a girl and Bubba has a boy and two girls, he started before I did, I think that's why.

I was the lover and Bubba was the tag-a-long, Bubba was a very costly best friend at times, but he could be a help too. He never knew how long to stay away from the car, I wanted to kill him a few times. Bubba would give you the shirt off his back though if he thought you needed it, but I couldn't get the point across to him that he wasn't staying gone long enough for me to get the shirt off my back.

Bubba just couldn't hardly stand being by himself I sometimes wondered if he was afraid of the dark. He just kept coming back to the car at short intervals. One morning after we had been out the night before Bubba said, I didn't know that girl you went out with last night was one eyed. We picked her up after dark and I didn't see her face until I came back to the car at nine-thirty. Jim Claude that has got to be the ugliest woman I believe I have ever seen, man you sure can pick'em.

After Bubba quit school he had to find a job an enter the world of labor. He got him a job with Mr. George Hagnot feeding his hogs and driving a tractor. Bubba was right at home and knew exactly what to do. Bubba was a good farmer and a right fair mechanic too. He moved right on up the ladder at Mr. George Hagnot's farm made him a few bucks and bought himself a little farm of his own. He sure was proud of his new farm, he worked from sunup to sundown everyday that is until he married Helen Sue. Helen Sue being the strong lady that she is put a change to all that nonsense, she was interested in starting a family and did.

Billy Bob is now the mayor, self-educated. Bubba Joe is a farmer and father. I must say Bubba turned out to be a good father too, his boys want to ride the tractor with him all day long.

Myrtle Martha is still the towns busybody just a bit older, ninety-one to be exact and still writing the news. Letha Ellen Switcher works at the bank and a good teller. Ella Mae Pfleuger owns the Snack Shop now. Lila Emma Ruth moved her practice north to be with her relatives and we haven't heard from her since. As we expected Rafe and Rose Jean married, but he don't stay around much, poor Rose is a very lonely woman. Nobody knows what Rafe does for a living, but he sends plenty of money home for Rose to live on, he even bought her a nice cottage in the country. Poor Rose just sobs and says, money sure don't take the place of love.

This town sure is changing fast, Billy Bob has finally got a couple of factories in town and the residents are living better. Ella Mae is really bringing in the chips at the Snack Shop. She bounces around the customers all day watching everyone's coffee cup trying to keep them full of flavorful Folgers. She puts out a nice dinner and a great burger and she's got the best pies in town. If you are ever down this way drop in and tell her Jim Claude sent you. She has a catchy little saying up over her door, "If you're hungry, we'll feed you." Everyone lovingly calls her the business woman in an apron.

Our Librarian Sheryl Judy Washammer has just retired and I am sure it was a great relief for her. She has been directing the Library for twenty years now and done a great job, at least everyone thinks so but one or two. Some wanted the Library to operate as big business or like a big town Library and we just didn't have the people for that. Another sad thing was that they wanted to run off all the patrons the Library already had and get new ones, I think.

All these people didn't know the first thing about operating a Library and would get mad if you suggested it. Perhaps the new Librarian will bring it from 10 people a day to 100 in a town of 120 people the age to need a Library. Oh well stranger things have happened, I guess I don't know.

P.S. I heard a bank president say once that it was taking absolutely too long to teach his new lenders how to get money from the central bank on the borrowers signature!

CHAPTER EIGHT
Country Women

Bubba Joe and I were in City Hall the other day to pay our light bills when this lady came in that was talking faster than the wheels on a locomotive can turn. She was joking with the clerk about how much more light bills were today than when she first married. At least we thought she was joking, the hall clerk might have thought different, Bubba Joe winked at me and said, "ain't women something else"? They sure are Bubba Joe, why? Oh I don't know, they can be two completely different people in a matter of minutes, one minute they just make you mad all over and at the snap of your finger they can become so sweet you just want to eat'em up.

If you don't tell them everyday how lovely they are then you don't love'em. Then you got a tiger on your hands if you do tell them that and some times you just aren't ready for that. Then again, you can pat them on the hand when they are not in the mood for it, then once again you hear, is that all you can think about, sex, sex, sex. You men are all sex crazy, sex in the kitchen, sex on the front porch and sex in the barn, men are nothing but animals. Let man come up a little short of her expectations and you might hear something like, if you are planning on keeping me around ole boy you had better get your act together.

Women act like they don't care about it until they don't get what they want or if man is just having a bad day. The younger generation is a little different?!

Women change constantly and all the time surprising her man. She will tell you about how great the President is and after she has had time to call one of her friends who doesn't like him, she hates him and wouldn't vote for him for dog catcher. Aren't they just wonderful, never a dull moment.

A friend of mine once made the statement that women just don't have it all together. I have met one who does and she is the coordinator for a private transportation company. Now if anyone is in a position to hate men it would be her. They don't make them like her anymore. I am one of her drivers and I sure hope she doesn't flip out some day and shoot us all.

Bubba Joe was telling me about a women he knew once named Lea Lee Robards. She married a man named Robert E. Leigh and now her name is Lea Lee Leigh. Just thought I would give you something to think about the next time you have to spend 2 or 3 hours in your Doctor's office waiting to see him. If he and his nurse are both in his office looking over paperwork, it could be a while longer!

I know a woman who talks like a motorboat sounds and she thinks talking is why women were put on this earth. She concentrates on her conversations as if they were multi-million dollar sales presentations. I have never seen anyone work any harder at anything as she does talking. When she is engaged in a conversation everything else becomes a government job and she puts her mind to nothing else. If she lays down her car keys, make-up case or ten bags of groceries while she is talking they become lost. I don't know how, but unless she or I get lucky they stay lost, bet she hasn't had to have over ten sets of keys made for her new car.

Most ladies love a phone almost as much as they do money, and more than hubby. Bubba Joe said, that man gets moved to the back burner when the phone rings. Hubby isn't even thought of anymore until the phone quits ringing long enough for her to become bored. It doesn't work to get in bed at twelve o'clock and wait on her to come to bed. Shucks, she may not come to bed before three AM. You can't even keep the thought up that long much less anything else, but I'll bet she wants to know why you were not awake.

Billy Bob (our mayor) was the first in town to get his wife one of these new cell phones. He couldn't find her for the first five days, he said she was in the house some place, he just didn't know where. When he finally found her she was ragged, torn and dirty, but she had the cell phone figured out. We heard that she lost ten pounds the time she was gone learning her new package. It was according to the Mayor; one of those new fangled jobs, the kind that old people never get figured out and throw away.

Bubba's wife use to have a dog and was crazy about it. It was a tiny little thing Bubba said, wasn't big as a bar of soap. It was short haired and brown, I guess you know that translates to ugly little rascal. He reported that it wasn't big enough to be good for anything but to lay around taking up space and biting you on the ankle at night when you stepped on him. We knew he was a dog Bubba said, but he didn't and the rascal could cause more trouble than a pack of wolves.

Bubba talked about how crazy she was over the mutt until he left her for another woman. Now if that had of been me she would have gotten out the ole 12 gauge, but she just talked all the time about him going to live somewhere else, like I wanted to hear it.

When Bubba's daughter got married her and his new son-in-law moved in with Bubba for two years. When they left the dog went with them, good riddance Bubba rejoiced.

The mutt had become too well thought of anyway Bubba lamented, He had already taken over my place in bed and moved me to the spare bedroom. The little sucker has always had more luck with women than I have. When company comes they just ooooh and aaaah over him like he was a good looking rich Jew. The dog just wagged his tail and licked their hand, wonder what would have happened if I had licked their hand? Some one else would probably be combing my hair, for the last time. No matter, I let him stay there anyway.

I reckon women and marriage just go together. Marriage down South is a little different however, than marriage in the North. As long as I can remember the men down South rule the roost. They are the boss, support the family, make the plans, decide who is doing what, who and when they were going to visit and how long they were going to stay. Women just washed, cooked, mended the clothes and had babies. The men also decided when she would have the babies and how large the family would be. Then sometimes when they were not pregnant the men would allow them to go to the field to chop or pick cotton for a change. Now the women were really thankful to get out of the house, but there was a problem with that, sometimes women would have to go to the woods for the bathroom and get lost. Some were never heard of again, must have gotten lost really deep in the woods.

Then one day my wife told me that some of the southern men were beginning to do things a little different, like in the North. Men were actually letting their wives start make some of the decisions, a little crazy don't you think? Well news kept coming south so fast that within a couple of years the women were trying to take over. Women now want to give the orders, spend the money, buy the groceries where they can cook for other men and women, once a month. The want to get the visiting set-up during the week where you are gone all week-end and never get any rest.

Does that make any sense at all?

Now she thinks she is in charge of when we work and when we play. Well fellows you know what I say, I say if they don't get back in line, we cut'em off. Cut'em off completely, that'll teach'em. We are just going to have to get tough and teach them that this ain't the North.

How many of you men had the task of teaching your wife how to drive? This is an undertaking for a real psychologist, not one of these throw them out they are too dumb to learn psychologist I mean a real one. Put your foot on the brake and pull down on the gear shift. Which one is the gear shift, screeeech, oh that must be it. I said, put your foot on the brake not the gas pedal.

That is the way it will be until she learns enough to let her go. You may not trust her, but you have come so close to dying so many times, that you just let her go.

Teaching your wife to drive is where most men learn to pray.

You learn very quickly that cursing doesn't work so you go to talking to God. I am sure God isn't very pleased at this and lets you sweat a little. Then after a while he realizes that you need mercy and lets you out of the mess you got yourself into. You then solemnly promise yourself that you will never undertake that job again and you hire someone to teach your daughter.

Your daughter, a whole new football field. Bubba Joe comes in one evening and Helen Sue tells him he needs to go upstairs and talk to his daughter. What do I need to talk to her about Helen Sue?

Well she is having girl problems. Helen Sue you got to be totally nuts, you think I am going up and talk to her about female problems? Well Bubba she is crazy about you and will listen to what you say. Yeah I'm sure she is going to listen to a man talk about something he knows nothing about. No way Helen Sue that is your job. Bubba left and went back to the field and worked all night by head lights.

P.S. Country women are beginning to get the idea that they are to become lovers not cooks!

Chapter Nine
Children

We Southerner are sure enough proud of our children down here, but we have our problems just like the North. We have to watch our children close when they are growing up. They don't grow up hardly as fast down here, we are a little slower paced. We have to be a little slower paced, because we are raising up the next generation of politicians. We going to get all the politicians in office from the South and our secret plans are to take over the North. We sure do hate to do it that way, because we may hurt a few Yankee's feelings, but we just don't have any choice.

If we leave the North in charge they are going to keep on with all this new fangled electric stuff and blow up America, see what I mean. We are going to do our best not to hurt any of them though. Rafe is heading up this operation and we done told him that we ain't going to hurt nobody. He agreed, he ain't come out of the barn yet, but he is still human too.

We got all our kids in school, we make them get their homework and require they go to the Library three times a week and play with them computers. Sometimes were will even carry them in the pick-up where they won't have to walk. We have to work hard down here in the South, but we try to be good to our children. They are good to us and do their chores so we owe them.

Mother even gives them some baked goods a couple times a week.

I got two children myself and it sure was hard to get them of age to be able to take care of themselves. My son is now thirty one and my daughter is twenty six. My son has four children two boys and two girls and my daughter has two boys. So in the wind up I got six grandchildren and my son and my daughter got hell to pay.

I am constantly kidding my youngest grandson about being a little girl. So this afternoon he called me a little girl and I said. You don't even know what a little girl is. Uh-huh I do to he says. I asked him what was the difference in a little boy and a little girl. I know he said, so I said no you don't, because you can't even tell me. Paw Paw I know the difference in a boy and a girl. What is it I asked? And he says, well a little girl don't have a zipper. So you see we are raising them right in the South.

We think we know all about love when we get married. We are old pros by the time we have been married six months, if we last that long. Then our children come along and teaches us what love is really all about. Over our children people who have never had a dispute or a fight become fighters. It has been heard about people becoming killers over their children. Children has a way of bringing the animal out in parents. I heard one mother say if she were an old sow she would just eat them. I Heard another mother say. she would eat anyway just to get rid of the evidence if she had enough nerve to whack'em over the head like she threatened a million times.

We love them however, we work our life away for them, we do without for them and then they repay us when they grow up, ha.

Billy Bob says that Trace Richard has repaid him ten times over, but Trace seems to think repay means something else. Trace ask him once, Pappy Bob haven't I given you loads of joy, you have to finish repaying me for that first, then when you get old I repay you.

When poor Billy Bob tells that story he just shakes his head and cries.

My daughter wanted me to buy her a car and I told her that I didn't have the money. She ask, Daddy you still have a checkbook don't you? I think I missed just a little with the concept of money lessons. And then she said, you still love me don't you Daddy, well that one almost got me. I almost went out and spent my last dollar that day and if I had I really don't suppose it would have mattered. These children sure do have a way of getting to your heart.

I tried for a long time to convince my son that he should go to college and he really didn't want to go. Then one day all of a sudden he wanted to go. We got him all fixed up at a college in Nashville and off he goes. Cost me a bundle. Then he had to have an apartment, then he had to have a car, Then he had to have money to eat on and last he had to have a little for pocket change. His concept of pocket change varied a long way from mine, as a matter of fact me, my wife and daughter was living on less than his idea of pocket change. He got bored having less to run around on than the other guys and came home in three months. I sure am glad it didn't take him three years to decide that. The family would have probably been living on dog food by then. Of course water would have been free excluding the electric bills. I could have gotten it out of the river or one of John Wayne's horse hooves.

If you remember in my first book FRONT LINE I told you what my son ask me about the popular vote. Children don't miss much that is going on in their local settings. You can think their mind is miles away and probably be right, but their ears are still there and missing nothing. You can use an uncolorful word and they got it. You can bet your largest farm in Georgia you are going to hear it again, vividly.

One of our local farmers Bobby Joe Harris drinks a couple of beers occasionally, just two a night. Well every night he had to go to our town convenience store to buy him two budweiser beers. One day he got tired of going everyday and just bought him a case and hid it in the barn. He had to go to Nashville for a couple of days and while he was gone the neighborhood kids found his stash and drank it all up. It of course made them drunk and happy so the kids raised a lot of commotion around the neighborhood. When Bobby Joe came home he had a couple of fences to fix and some tall explaining to do. I felt sorry for him because Bobby Joe's a good ole boy, but it taught him a lesson, he back to driving to town every night.

We learn early down south, never try to second guess a kid 'cause you never know what they are going to do.

P.S. Somebody ought to shoot the guy who taught the kids what a cop is!

CHAPTER TEN
How We Look At The Government

When I was a child growing up they always counted the votes by hand. It always took a few days to get the count, but you never heard of anyone getting upset because they didn't think the votes were counted right.

So then some one who wasn't quite right upstairs came up with the electoral vote. It was set up so that each state got x amount of electoral votes' according to the size and number of residents of each state, now that's my college kicking in here. There were probably two or three more things that were used in rigging up the electoral for each state, but I don't know they are. Seems you never get the whole picture where the white house is concerned. That's the reason for two or three thousand people up there milling around every day, keeps everyone confused, everyone.

The government's computer plays a big part right here, they break down the electoral votes per candidate. If Oregon had 70 electoral votes and sixty per-cent of the people voted for Bush and 60 per-cent voted for Clinton it would be broken down like this. Bush would get 50 electoral votes and Clinton would get 20. Now that's fair enough, isn't it. Maybe its not fair, I don't know!

The other guy, what's his name, Al Gore would have found something wrong with it if it had been the other way. I got a feeling that Flipper would not have let him go along with any results. Here is a girl that may some day be President, it would not surprise me in the least. You think Hillary is a sharp lady, it is a strong possibility that you ain't seen nothing yet. Tipper probably has the answer for America's insurance problem already, but holding on to it for the time being until everything is just right. Bubba Joe says, she would be the best looking President ever.

Poor Al didn't get to raise much racket while he was Vice did he? Clinton kept him on special assignments and on overseas missions seems like all the time. Every time Al tried to make a speech on TV Clinton would have him mysteriously whisk away on another special mission. Poor man spent half his time on an airplane going somewhere. Clinton had a special plane made for him, I think, with one of his offices on the plane where he would have a place to write his message to where ever he was going. What surprised me was Billy Bob said the reason for Clinton keeping him out of the country all the time was that Clinton was afraid Al would sneak Monica Lewinski from under his nose. What do you think?

Last week I went to pay my light bill and didn't have enough money to pay it. So I ask Billy Bob about what to do since he is a money genius. Do you suppose Bush would forgive me the debt since I am a good citizen I asked? I kinda doubt it was Billy Bob's response. Well I don't see why not it is only forty dollars and he or someone forgave Russia a seven hundred billion dollar grain debt I told Billy Bob. Russia is one of our neighboring countries though reported Billy Bob, and it sure was a big help to get them out of debt to us. Well that was an expensive price for allegiance I told , heck I would have been his ally for forty bucks and from the looks of things he probably would have been just as well off.

I don't know, I guess I just don't understand these government people. They tell you what you want to hear one day, something different the next day and then start a war the next day. I could have solved the problem back in 1990 if they would have just called on me, but no they wanted to mess it up good as usual.

I would have got me a bunch of boys off of death row, trained them up better than the Geneva Force and sent them over with the instructions that when every one of the Saadam bunch was dead they would have a pardon. I would have named it Operation Blue Tick. I would have had them some shoulder patches made up with the picture of a Blue Tick Hound on them, tearing out Saadam people throats. Sure would have been good for their moral.

The numbers sure do fit better to me, kill 30 guilty people to save thousands innocent lives. Does that make sense to you, maybe I am wrong. I guess sometimes us Southerners just go on a kill spree. It sure would not have been like the war between the states.

We felt kinda sorry for our National brothers from the North. Just because our leaders were a little mad at each other we didn't see any need in trying to kill off all the poor people, they couldn't help it because our leaders didn't have any more sense than to get mad at each other like that.

We know America that you people up North may be a little more highly schooled than we are. We know you think us a little dumb because we live a little bit back in the woods, sticks as some call it. And some of us live a pretty fer piece back in the woods, but we want to get this clear right now. We want you to know what we believe and what we don't believe.

What we believe is that all them government men we voted for to represent us in Washington have our best interest at heart. If one of them gets up and says he is going to work for the farmers then we believe he is going to work for the farmers. We believe they are good ole boys and would give you the shirt off their backs if they thought you needed it. Now that is what we believe northern boy.

What we don't believe is that they look down their noses at us just because they are richer than us. We don't believe they get bills passed to make money. We don't believe that they will go buy stock in a large company and then get a bill passed that will insure the increase of the products so they can come home richer. We don't believe that any of them would borrow money from some rich overseas family and then let the price of gas go from $1.30 to $3.00 a gallon just to line their pockets. We may be thought dumb down here, and maybe we ain't as smart as some, but we ain't idgits. Bubba Joe said it just made him sick how they made fun of us Southerners.

Billy Bob called me two days ago and said he had watched the news and heard one of the Senators say that he was going fighting the next morning at a meeting. He said he was going to get some price hikes for farm products. I never heard from Billy Bob about that subjects, but I did my wife. She went to buy groceries the next day and sure enough the prices on cereal and sausage was up thirty cents. I do have to admit that the gentleman kept his word. Billy Bob ain't eat no sausage since, bless his heart.

I keep harping on the government about sending factories overseas, have you ever heard of anything that stupid. Sending our job market to China, Japan and God knows where else. These guys are cutting their own throats, because one day in the near future there will be none here with enough money to buy their products and they will run whining to the government again. Cheaper will hold no value then and they will have to lower end item prices.

If that's not bad enough, a great number of factories are going to Mexico. We already have half of Mexico's work force in America, illegally. Then they are sending enough factories down there to employ the rest of them. It sure does look like who ever is heading up this plan for a one world government is an idiot. A full fledge- number one- died in the wool idiot, but there is nothing unusual about that, I don't think.

That would be like sending all the septic tanks to Puerta Rico and then bringing all the septic tank cleaners up to America.

Then you would end up with all the product in one place and all the ----

In the other. Perhaps that might make more sense than you think.

Billy Bob, our mayor, goes to a lot of these political meeting in Nashville. He says he really enjoys listening to those political guys speak, because they use so many big words and all. One of the town business men was in Nashville at the same time as Billy Bob was. Billy Bob and his office girl went off to hear some of those speakers at a big state gathering. The neighbor came back telling that the real reason that Billy Bob like going was the Nashville Hilton. He told that the day he was there that Billy Bob and his office girl never got out one time the whole day.

Some of the town people ask Billy Bob about that and he denied it. The mayor said he had no time for another woman that his office girl was a little sick that day and he had to stay in and take care of her! He said, "Now folks I want you all to know that I have no desire for any of that eatra-circular activity, I am very happy with the woman I got, my wife. He said that it was senseless to go out and spend a lot of money like that when you got a sure thing at home. Billy Bob's wife said that it was senseless to put out a lot of extra effort on a tite-wad ole man, too. So I guess what's up is up and what's down is down, I don't know for sure.

P.S. No one knew until it was too late that Al Gore's most special assignment was NAFTA!

CHAPTER ELEVEN
The Invitation

I have never understood why the South was limited to just a few Southern states. I know it is going to be boring, but I want you to know what I mean, here we go: Alabama, Georgia, Tennessee Mississippi, Missouri, Arkansas, Louisiana and Texas. North and South Carolina are on the same level as Tennessee and Georgia, but no not the same.

There is Oklahoma, New Mexico and Arizona, but no they are western states. Virginia is New England, Kentucky is something and Kansas is part of the North. I don't understand maybe we just got our own little clique down here. It can't be just the way we talk, its got to be something else. I know we are unique, but so is everybody. I know we are a handsome lot and sexy is a way of life down here, but what is the real reason. We are getting a lot of the North's factories, but so is China and they ain't popular. I know there is a lot of orange trees down South, but Florida ain't one of us because of Bush's brother. Anyway if you should figure it out, do let us know.

We would like to invite you South for a visit or to live either one. There is plenty of open land to build you a house and it is all breathtaking scenery. If you decide to come for a visit bring at least three thousand dollars for every week you are going to stay, because we are planning on getting at least that much. We got to keep everything up to par for the next visitor you know. If you are planning on moving here to stay, be a millionaire or be prepared to work. We don't need bums or beggars and we sure don't need anyone looking for welfare, we got enough of our own.

Don't bring your daughter if she is sexually active because we have quit supporting the baby havers and are putting that money on the roads. We are blacktopping the road just up from my house right now, it takes millions. However if you have a daughter that is not into that we sure do need some more fast food waitresses. We could use a few more honest people in our nursing homes, hospitals and Wal-Marts. One of our sister towns is getting a new wal-marts as we speak.

If you are Mexican feel free to come there is a load of construction jobs here. Our local boys won't do that type of work unless it is in a supervisory position. Sorry, but their jobs in supervision has been long since gone.

If you are Iranian, don't bother. The governments going to give you enough money to buy a motel or convenience store anyway. They won't loan us Southern boys money to start a business on, but all you have to do is ask. Looks like we may have to go to Australia and start building roads and businesses out back.

I wonder if those furners have to pay any taxes?

We don't have any mountains around here in Tennessee, but we are not looking for any full timers anyway in Tennessee just rich visitors. I can't answer for the surrounding States, but I'm sure they have a website where you can get all the answers. The web is a little different below the Mason Dixon so venture slowly.

Although you have been invited to the South, don't come down here looking for a wife. We don't have any women to spare. Besides our women have heard stories about men from the north and I think they have made up their minds to stay home with the Southern boys. I don't mean to hurt your feelings, but I can't control the Southern girls either. We don't have enough chickens to feed you all either, ain't hardly none of them laying so breakfast would be slim. It ain't easy to feed a family of eleven or twelve and then have a bunch of company coming. If you decide to come visiting, send Nashville a letter at least two weeks ahead, let us get prepared. Preciate it.

Hope when you do come for a visit, your dog has just run away from home. Tennessee got a lot of extra ones and need a place for them. We will send food for the first year, if you take one back with you. We send it by the month, but will try not to get behind. We have to have time to dry the possum meat Bobby Joe catches in his traps, then we have to bag it.

Them dogs love dried possum though, they will chase you all over the horse lot for it. If they catch you then you better be prepared for a fight, but I don't care nothing about it anyway I just let'em have it bless their hearts. You got any dogs, yard dogs I'm talking about, them kind big enough to go out there in the woods and catch critters. Ain't they lovable, they will bring in the bacon and then watch over it until you get time to skin it for Mammy to cook.

I like working dogs the best like them critter dogs we was just talking about. I never could care for them teeny weenys. Why the ain't big enough to be good for anything, they are all the time in the way. My friend Bubba Joe calls them woman dogs, cause women just go nuts over them. I don't know why I ain't never seen enough there to get crazy over. Women will follow them around all evening with a food and water bowl trying to get them to eat. Now if we could just get them to follow us around with a wash rag and try to keep the yuk from between our toes, we might be able to accept them little mutts better. I don't know, maybe I'm wrong.

I hate cats, they give me shivers, they are nasty looking, nasty smelling, they got to have a box to poop in, the foul smelling creatures. They eat nasty things, too like mice, birds, baby ground hogs and them little things that dig tunnels in the ground. My daddy hated cats, but my wife taught me different.

Now that I have invited you to come south for a visit, I sure hope a lot of you all will come on down and bring lots of money with you. The town mayor suggested that I put in here what I have about the money. He says we sure need it that Tennessee and Georgia are going broke.

Georgia has still got her peaches to rely on and Tennessee ain't got nothing to rely on, volunteer states don't have nothing. I wonder how many bushels of peaches Georgia sells a year. Probably 450 maybe 500 bushels a year, why everybody in America could have a peach and there would still be some left over.

Approximately 50 years ago America got on this spraying kick. Almost everything is sprayed in America now, they say it makes things last longer, maybe it does. They spray fruits and vegetables except for the human kind. They spray grass, mosquitoes, almost all animals are sprayed for ticks dogs, cats, horses. They spray houses, barns, pig pens, what a world. Women spray on suntans, make-up, medicines everything but spray on hair. There is stuff to spray on their hair, but nothing to spray the hair on so I guess these bald headed people just going to have to be satisfied with no hair. They got these rugs, but you are better off with no hair.

Bubba Joe was trying to put on a tie yesterday to go to a funeral. H tried 6 or 7 times with no luck so he yelled for his wife. She came in and tied his tie for him first try. That makes me mad Bubba Joe said as many times as I tried to tie that thing and failed. His wife grinned at him and says, it just takes a woman's touch. As she left the room she ran into the dresser and knocked off her prize lamp and it broke into a hundred pieces and Bubba Joe said, a woman's touch.

Alfred Joe Horner told Bubba Joe that his wife went off to see her mother a few weeks ago, that she hadn't see her in six years. Bubba said, I sure hope she had a good visit with her mother. She did Alfred said, but she had to cut her visit short because her dog fell and broke his hip. She came home early to see about her dog and take care of him. She said she didn't trust me to take care of him.

Bubba laughed and reported that women were crazy creatures, like were weren't aware. They will threaten to kill you oveer nothing and come home a week early from a trip three thousand miles to take care of a dog, over nothing. I'll make you think over nothing Bubba Joe Pierce, yelled Helen Sue, why I oughta scalp you. You're just an over grown lug is what you are, with no feelings whatsoever.

Mrs. Peckinpaugh was trying to get a peanut butter jar open yesterday the new teacher was telling us. She could unscrew the lid with her hand so her tried holding the lid with her teeth. Poor lady is getting on up their and had just put a new batch of polygrip on her teeth. She got the lid hung in her teeth and they had to take her to the doctor to get it out, but she was lucky. The doctor got so tickled and had such a great time out of it that he didn't charge poor Mrs. Pechinpaugh a thing.

Seems like when it rains it pours, no sooner did Mrs. Peckinpaugh get home Pop Washammer got into trouble. Pop is Jim's dad and Sheryl Judy said that he was going to bed for a nap that afternoon and when he was taking his britches off as he always did, he got the zipper hung and couldn't get his pants off. He had to crawl through his britches leg to get them danged things off, she chirped. Now Pop's a character he sings all the time and whistles the rest, he chews apple chewing tobacco and can hit a five gallon bucket from thirty feet. Pop got his zipper hung once before when he was seventy, serious he had to go to the doctor over that one.

Pop use to be quite a squirrel hunter they tell me. Said he stayed in the woods most of the time back then. The story was told that he went hunting one Sunday afternoon and didn't get home until Saturday night at six o'clock. He brought home thirty squirrels and said if he hadn't run out of apple tobacco he would have stayed another week. H couldn't understand why his wife was upset with him, he said she had plenty of food to eat. If there hadn't been no grub in the house I might could have understand Mama's griping, he argued.

Mama ain't no saint Pop said. She got mad at me last Sunday morning and told me to get out of the house, that she wasn't going to be cooking me no supper for a week. So I figured I might as well be out laying up a little fresh squirrel meat for when she did start cooking again. Bubba Joe ask him why she got that mad at him and Pop said, ah you know how women are they want what they want when they want it and what they don't want is excuses, and heck Bubba Joe I'm eighty nine years old, I ain't no young man no more and Mama don't understand that. Shucks man, I had to slow down some when I got eighty five, ain't no sprang chicken.

Mama Washammer just continued to rock and pat her foot and spit rooster snuff off the end of the porch. I got the impression it wasn't over by no means.

Mama Washammer was eighty four her last birthday, but still mighty spry for her age. She was a mid-wife until she was seventy and very good at it I hear tell. Martha Ann and Mavis Anne were both delivered by Mama Washammer and a whole bunch more. Some babies she delivered she has out lived by quite a spell and Mama still grieves for them all. Mama is quite a woman and a good one, too. Mama is best known for her blackberry cobbler, most people would walk a country mile for just one small serving of her cobbler, mouth watering.

Speaking of mouth watering, Sheryl Judy Washammer can make the most scrumptious caramel pie you ever laid upon a taste bud. The crust is flaky an crunchy and the pie filling is so good it just makes your taste buds fight to see who will get the most. Sheryl Judy has been making pies of all kinds for a lot of years and that is why she is so good at it. Anybody in the neighborhood gets sick she makes them a pie and takes it to them. We seem to have had an over abundance of sickness in our neighborhood the last few years. Sheryl just may have spoiled these people, what do you think? Sheryl said if she had a nickel for every pie she had made that she could build her a new home. It ain't gone unnoticed by Jim's checkbook.

CHAPTER TWELVE
Looking Back

Looking back over the few years I have lived here I can remember a lot of things and they were all good. Even though I had of rather lived in the mountains, the Ozarks preferably I have had a good life and a lot of fun. I have worked like a dog to present my wife and two children with as good a living as I could, but it has been a pleasure. I am sixty four retired, overweight, and called comfortable now instead of sexy, but it was wonderful and I must thank my God for that. He has watched over me and made my life profitable and some thing to cherish, but he didn't let me go to the mountains. So ya'll got to buy lots of these books so I can go as often as I wish.

I remember as a young man I started out as a painter and worked most of the time, from the beginning I was a good painter and everyone was satisfied with my work. I always put plenty of paint on the walls to make it look rich and deep. Then I added plumbing and it didn't take me long to realize it wasn't my cup of tea, Then came electrical and last carpentry. I became good at all of these and provided the country with a good contractor. I never lost but $150.00 the whole time I was a contractor(30 years). Pretty good record wasn't it?

I remember I was out driving around one Sunday afternoon and got lost. I kept driving wishing I could start recognizing something. Then I noticed something across the fence, it was a girl and she was a mess. She had on overalls and brogans and her hair was an absolute mess. She had mud on her face and a big bump beside her nose. She smiled but kept shying away from me just as if she thought I might hurt her, After an hour I finally convinced her I was alright, but she hadn't said a word yet. I don't guess she had ever seen a car, because she kept rubbing mine smiling at it and humming, still not a word. I finally got her in the car and got her home by her pointing out the directions.

Pulled up in the yard and Papa Warner her Dad with shotgun and six hound dogs met me at the porch. What you want boy he said? I just brought your daughter home sir she looked like she was lost. My daughter wasn't lost he said, she knows this country like the back of her hand.

She had disappeared, but showed up soon with her face washed, a clean dress on and smiling constantly. I stayed talking to her Papa Warner as long as possible. Then for some reason I heard myself asking him if I could come back and see his daughter. He smiled and ask, reckon yall git married? Well I don't know I don't know if she will even like me or not. Well come on back boy and court her if you must, but be good 'cause I will be watching you and one wrong move hot shot and you'll be hog feed.

So I dated her for a couple years with Papa Warner telling me all the time, ya'll got to git married boy, cause I'm getting tired of watching you. I was not sure that Papa Warner ever knew my name

Until a few years later he started calling Uncle Jim.

Then we ask him if we could get married and he hung his shotgun up and told me I had better take good care of her and don't ever think you are going to send her back home or I'll get ole Jackson there off the rack again, and if I do things ain't going to be pretty. Not for you anyway. We been married forty two years now and I have never the first time had the desire to send her home. I have thought about killing her a few times, but never sending her home. Besides she loves me too much, I know because she said she did. And I have not forgotten Jackson or where he hangs, Her Dad may be 85 but he ain't dead.

Once in the heat of passion she told me what she really thought of me, boy was she mad. I learned early to watch out for her right especially when the phone receiver was in it. Her right foot is wicked also and I do mean wicked. It don't ask where it can kick, it just whales away at it and never off target. Papa Warner told me I had more to contend with here and just didn't know about it yet. Boy you got some coming to grips to do, Papa laughed.

Well we got married and I went off to the Army an agreement between me and Sheryl Judy. She said she didn't want to be right in the middle of having our first baby and the army call me. I guess that was right sensible in her way of thinking. She said it would be like the army to wait until she was having a baby or I got my first pickup truck and made four payments. Then the poor ole pickup would have to sit right there in the same spot until I got back. My girl really looks ahead.

I came home and got out of the army and we moved back to West Tennessee, best place on the map. We bought us a little spot of land with a house, barn, corn crib and a chicken house an a big ole red oak stump already on it. It wasn't on a hill even though I had always said that when I bought myself a house it was going to be on a hill. It would have been too, but Sheryl Judy said no the pickup might roll down the hill backards into the neighbors house. Then there would go your brand new pickup with four payments made and the neighbors house.

I told her that we could just buy some insurance on the house and the truck. She laughed, now ain't that just like you Jim Claude, you know we would have to buy the insurance from Billy Bob and if anything happened Billy Bob would find a way to collect the insurance money. Besides she reasoned, I ain't never trusted these insurance companies no further than I could throw a cow by the tail. Its sort of like these doctors telling you to take two aspirins and call'em in the morning, all they want is your money. You know, sometimes my Sheryl Judy makes some pretty good sense. I didn't push the idea any further, because I wasn't to excited about having to insure the neighbors house on Sheryl Judy's assumption that the truck was going to roll backards down the hill.

Then we met Bubba Joe and Helen Sue Pierce, our first neighbors. We liked them right off and knew that we were really going to enjoy living close to them. Sheryl Judy said that she trusted Bubba Joe because he didn't have that little line going down his forehead. Bubba Joe does seem like a nice guy I said, and on top of that Helen Sue has a shapely little backside. Then and there was the first time that Sheryl Judy ever hit me with telephone receiver. I don't understand these women they don't seem to know when a man is joking. No sense of humor!

Bubba Joe and Helen Sue always had a lot of company in those days and Alford Joe was probably his best friend at that time. Alford Joe was visiting him one weekend and Bubba ask him how all the family in Memphis were doing. Alford said, he didn't know about everybody else, but it seemed to him his whole family had been sick for a month. Even my dog he said, the little rascal fell last week and broke his hip.

My wife's grandmother was trying to put some peanut butter on crackers and was having a lot of trouble getting the lid off the jar. She finally put the lid in her mouth so she could twist with both hands, guess what? She got the blooming lid hung in her false teeth and they had to take her to the Doctor to get it unstuck.

Then my Grandpa got up to go to bed last Wednesday night and when he started to take his pants off he got the zipper hung. In the wind up he had to crawl through his britches leg to get his pants off. Almost broke his leg making the turn!

Patty Mae got that upset stomach that is going around and threw up for two days last week. Patty Mae had two green bowls setting on the table and one was full of chicken salad and the other was empty. She threw up in the empty bowl and ran off to the bathroom to clean up a little and when she got back she couldn't tell which was which and had to throw them both away. Ruin some of the best chicken salad you could ever get.

Now me I got up early Friday morning with an awful cough that just kept getting worse all day long. By the time I got ready to go to bed I coughed so hard I jarred my earring out of my tongue and swallowed it. I have been sick ever since. Every one of us had to go the doctor last week. I tell you Bubba Joe, last week was murder.

According to Bubba Joe, Alford had a hard life growing up. He had to start picking cotton when he was six years old. His daddy would hook up the german shepard to Alford's home made wagon, not a red wagon it was brown, and Alford would pick cotton and fill up the brown wagon because he was too little to pull a cotton sack.

After it got too dark to pick cotton Alford had to feed the hogs and chickens while his daddy milked and fed the cows and bull. Alford gets a kick out of telling about his daddy going to milk the cows one night after dark. His Dad got the bull mixed up with one of the cows and put the bull into one of the milking stalls. Alford Joe gets to laughing so hard all he can say after that is that, they came to a quick understanding.

Poor Alford didn't have enough room to sleep in the house with his ten brothers and sisters, so he had to sleep under the front porch.. He said, he started out sleeping on the porch, but it was so hard and the hound dogs looked like they were resting real nice like, so he just moved under the porch with them. It was just a little dustier than Alford liked so he put him some hay under the porch to sleep on. The very first night he had to fight every one of them hounds to get his bed back.

Alford survived it pretty well though, the only two real scars it left on him is that he tends to crawl around in tight places and the way he scratches.

The next summer I planted my first garden. Sheryl Judy liked the idea, said she would cook from it and can what was extra in mason jars. Her mother must have taught her to put up canned food because every night she kept me busy breaking green beans and shelling purple hull peas. She would tell me that when I got the peas shelled and ready for canning that she would have my supper ready, not before. During the following winter I sure was happy that I had put in all those hours preparing vegetables. Now let me tell you my friend, I still hate shucking and silking sweet corn.

We still didn't have any children yet, so I went in one evening and told Sheryl Judy that we had to soon start working on getting us some kids. I know she remarked, but we got to get them two hounds out yonder grown first. Sheryl Judy what in this world has those two hounds got to do with getting kids? Jim Claude sometimes I believe you are totally nuts. We are learning how to do it right with them hounds, that way when we get kids and raise them we will already know how its done and won't make any mistakes. So much for Sheryl Judy making sense, but we do love our hounds.

Then we met the Billy Bob Hagnot family, a hard working farmer at the time. His wife I thought must have been French because she had the funniest name. Juliana Diana Hagnot was the first woman I ever met with that name. Hagnot was common enough, there is Hagnots all over Tennessee, but that Juliana Diana is what threw me. Sheryl Judy told me not to be pickin at her about her name and I agreed. Then she ran off with that carpenter and forced Billy Bob into being what he is today. Been knowing Billy Bob forty years since his wife left and ain't known him to hit a lick of work since. He said, everyone else is, so I might as well have a slice of the pie. Sheryl Judy sure was shocked at his new attitude.

Sheryl and I have really enjoyed our little place in the world for the last forty years. We live one mile from Sheryl's family where she can go there three or four times a day. And I have been sitting on my front porch after work every afternoon for the past forty years dreaming about moving to the mountains. I probably wouldn't have enough steam to climb one of them little suckers now if I got to move there, so here we are. I might even miss this place if we were to leave it, for thirty minutes or so anyway, I don't know.

I feel sort of left out sometimes, Sheryl has forty six girlfriends and I only got one! Sheryl really has a big time with them they have at least one party a week, pot luck, presents and the whole nine yards. Sheryl is really good to me though she leaves me a batch of tuna salad and a gallon of iced tea in the frig so I won't get hungry. I have had the life of a king here though so I got nothing to gripe about. I would go a long way to make sure Sheryl Judy is happy.

Sheryl is wanting to move up town with them hifalooten people, so I guess we will go. She says she can walk up town from that retirement complex when she gets mad at the mayor and give him a little piece of her mind. They just might straighten him out though I know I sure would hate to look up and see twelve gray headed angry women coming into my office. Billy Bob sure has got a lot to look forward to from here on.

Sheryl Judy is a member of that red hat society, what ever that is. I'm not sure but I think it is a group of retired women that goes around making waves for the common town people. They wear purple dresses and red hats, all kind of hats. I saw a bit on the news about them once, thirty six of them and I ain't never seen so many different hats in my life. There was big ones, little ones, tall one, short ones, hats with brims, hats with no brims, with bands, without bands, it was frightening. If I had to be around that many hats and that much noise I would go completely batty. I wonder what kind of shape that poor announcer is in. He may still be in the hospital.

Well first I retired and then went back to work on a retirement job and decided to write this book. So I now have three different things going at one time as many as I have ever had going at once and older than I have ever been. Mother nature has been good to me and let me reach this age gracefully. God was good to mother nature and told her it was okay. So at this age I have become hopeful, predictable and comfortable, but I am rich. I have a graceful loving God, a tolerant wife, a good family on both sides and a nice pickup with four payments made already.

Chapter Thirteen
Within Certain Limits

In one of our neighboring towns they have what they call the Badger Fight. Since the badger is one of the most dreaded animals of the South their fearless fighting tactics are avoided by most every animal. Under certain circumstances the badger has been known to attack man without fear and usually comes out the better of the two.

When someone new moves into this town all the townspeople get together and gives them sort of an initiation style welcome. So occasionally someone will stick their headed inside all the business houses and yells "badger fight fifteen minutes". This action usually set the town in an uproar.

The whole town gathers for the badger fight and nothing else goes on within the city limits until the badger fight is over. One of the business men has a hound specially trained for the fight using badger scents, he's a hideous thing. A dog that outweighs any other I have ever seen by fifty pounds, large jowls hangs halfway to the ground and he continuously foams at the mouth as though he is mad. He hates badgers with all of his canine heart and all he can think about is "kill that badger".

Whom ever the new addition to the town, is taken to the fight and given one end of a ten foot rope that comes from under the door of a shed which stands southerly and adjacent to the town cotton gin. He is told that when someone manages to get the shed door open that houses one of the largest badgers in the South, his job is to jerk that rope as hard as he can and jerk the badger out into the open. He is cautioned to give the jerk everything he has in order to be sure that he gets the animal outside the building. He was told that if the hound should manage to get loose and into the building with a badger that size the poor hound wouldn't have a chance, but outside he could kill the badger.

All this time the dog is smelling badger scent and going out of his mind. He is constantly jumping against the end of the rope with all his might, trying his best to get loose of the rope and to the shed where he smells the badger scent.

All of a sudden the door swings open and the designated man jerks the rope with all his might, but no badger, instead out comes a shiny white jenny kettle full of water, better known to southerners as a slop jar. As a result the newcomer is drenched, standing with water dropping from everywhere.

I have heard that sometimes the new man gets a little carried away and tries to kill every person in his sight. It at times takes four or five men to hold him until he cools off enough to see the fun in it. Some join in the fun, some move away and some just never seem to join the town people and become loners.

The strange welcome is then completed until another new family moves to town and has been going on for over a hundred years. " Badger Fight Fifteen Minutes".

Two years ago Billy Bob calls a special town meeting and invited all the town residents to come share their ideas and suggestions. This would have been a good idea for the town and ultimately Billy Bob would have gathered a wealth of good useable information. Something went wrong.

First thing Billy Bob knew the people had ventured onto the subject of Love. Bad move Billy Bob knew, because everyone have their own ideas about love. They blamed Alford Joe for getting it started but he passed the buck on to Rafe McCutson. So in the final decision by the people and for the people Rafe got the honors. The discussion goes on and if you had been their you would have heard more descriptions of love than you ever dreamed possible. I don't really think any of them made any sense, however Bubba Joe said, and made his point that love meant having two wallets. Each of the wallets described Bubba Joe have their purpose and very special purposes.

One of the wallets he chirped is the man's wallet used solely for the purpose to hold down hard feelings between lovers. The other is to keep money in to give to the wife for her use. Special uses such as Wal Mart, grocery store, Wal Mart, furniture store, Wal Mart, and any place that sells items that nick nacks that have no real value.

Oh yeah Alford Joe said, I sure learned my lesson from criticizing those type purchases. After we first married says he, my wife goes off to Wal Mart and comes back with the back seat of the car full of things she bought. There was one big bag full of things that I had no idea what they were. Regretfully I ask, what in the world is all this junk? This is not junk I have you know Alford this is a hot pad made like a glove. So I continued to stumble and ask, what in the world do you need that thing for. Well I can use it when I get me a Dutch Oven she reported and if I don't use it I can give it as a Christmas present. That is when I decided it was better just to shut up

The next day said Alford I learned lesson number two. I learned to say I am sorry every chance I got and pretend not to pay any attention to the fact that she never said I'm sorry. There is just something about saying your sorry to a woman that just really turns them on. My woman can cry louder than anyone I have ever heard. Oh you don't love me! I'm sorry dear. You think I am stupid and can't buy for the family! I'm sorry dear. You can just sleep on the couch for the next week! I'm sorry dear. I'm sorry, sorry, sorry.

If you say you are sorry often enough, always give them twenty dollars more than they ask for and never let them think that you think you are smarter than they are, then you have probably got a mate for life. The worst possible thing you can do is to let them know that you are smarter than they are. Men whether we like it or not we have got to act dumb.

Buy them jewelry by all means, it doesn't matter if it is fake just buy them jewelry. They will drive a car from the sixties as long as their neck, fingers and toes are shining. When they pass on you will have a pick up truck load of jewelry to do something with. You still may not have but four payments made on the truck but you will have enough jewelry to fill it.

Women are very loveable creatures at times and can bring you to the point of being a dangerous creature as well. Yon can go to bed with loving on your mind, kick off the starting line and really get into some serious moves. Right when you think you are heading for the goal post she says, sweetheart you are a wonderful kisser, but I have a splitting headache. You quickly come to the thought of splitting it for her. Then you calm down because you know you can't do without her. You just turn over mumbling erzch

Blitod cofja en gribbijch.

They can be scary too, if you don't think so just watch for who is driving the next car that tries passing a dozen times and when they finally get around you they hit their brakes and turn off. The reason you never noticed it was a woman is because you are doing everything you can think of including praying trying to keep your car on four feet. It also scare you to think about how your wife drives when she is out on the road, in heavy traffic. Women never think about having a wreck, just about getting in front. Billy Bob says that women and cars were just not made for each other, just women and hospitals.

You know I never really had time to talk to you about Trace Richard Yoder up until now. Trace Richard as you remember is

Billy Bob's son by his first marriage. His first wife was a Mennonite and probably a nice lady, but ole Billy Bob was fire on wheels when he was young. So I guess you can come up with where Trace Richard got his wildness.

Young Trace was so wild at an early age that he completely broke out of school young and refused to go back. Billy Bob could do nothing about it and down right give up on the boy. He grew up to be a teenager some how, but Trace seem to chill out just a little as he grew older.

My son was hanging out once with Trace and he was admiring Trace's new truck. He said Trace told him about a new cutting tool he had bought to cut his seat belt if he got caught up in it. My son ask to see it and Trace got it out of his tool box. Trace is a smart boy, eh. He put one of those chrome tool boxes on that green and pink four wheeled drive truck hes so crazy over. He said, it reminded him of putting bologna and lettuce together in a sandwich.

Trace bought him a guitar and a book of chords, but couldn't do any good at learning to play. He talked to everyone he met about giving him guitar lessons, but all he talked to put him off and Trace didn't learn. Trace put in hour after hour after hour on that guitar. Why I bet his fingers was as tough as a piece of leather. He could get some of the most foul sounding sounds out of that thing than I have ever heard before.

Finally in complete desperation he ask Rafe McCutson to give him a few guitar lessons, Rafe however was more interested in giving him a few other lessons, so poor Trace just gave up guitar. He said, if he had to go through all that to learn to play the guitar, he would just forget it.

I went to Domino's pizza parlor one night to get a pizza for supper and Trace was already there. They had completed his order and ask him if he wanted it sliced into 4 pieces or 6 pieces. Trace thought about it a few seconds and told them to cut in 4 pieces that he didn't think he was hungry enough to eat six pieces.

There was one thing that Trace was good at and that was sleight of hand. He could palm a half dollar even if it was two quarters and you would never know what he did or where it was. He went around showing all the kids what he could do and they followed him all over town. We never knew if they really liked him or if he was keeping their quarters.

Poor Trace everyone likes him, but I think he got hit on the head at some time or another. I sure can say one thing about Trace though, he sure ain't nothing like his Daddy, he will spend more money in a month that Billy Bob will in five years. Billy Bob loves him though, said he did!

Chapter Fourteen
The Corn Cob Festival

The town has been trying to come up with something for years, ever since Billy Bob got elected mayor, that would pull in out of town people. Them tourist would add a lot of revenue to this town Billy Bob claims. That would add more money to the local businesses and mean the opening of new businesses which would mean more tax money for our fair city.

Billy Bob called in some of his leading ladies along with the red hat society and put the burden on their shoulders. The best thing they could come up with was " The City Of The Flower Park." but Billy Bob was not at all happy with that, so he burdened them further. Oh he tried everything, ask everyone, but to no avail, seemed that no one could come up with anything that suited the mayor.

Billy Bob was so determined to get something going that he advertised in his small town for someone to come up with an angle to pitch to the world. There were many suggestions made, but Billy Bob said, " When the right thing comes along I will know, no I am sorry but I just can't use that". He kept making that statement until it exhausted everyone in town and the suggestions quit coming. So one day all out of the blue Trace Richard came in to Billy Bob's office and approached his Father, Paw, you been looking for something to build your town to the world, maybe I can help. What you got Trace? Nothing 'cause I ain't put my mind to it yet, but I will come up with something. OK Trace you come up with something an I will see if I can use it.

When Trace left Billy Bob said under his breath, I won't hear any more from him. Smiling he continued on his plight, he was a bit proud that Trace had been so attentive and wanted to help hi ole man out of a fix.

The next day Trace was back in his office with his first suggestion. Ok Trace what you got for your Father today, Billy Bob asked? Well, I was thinking on the way home yesterday, that maybe we could become Mennonites or Amish. We could have attractions about peoples nationality and I hear they are big coon hunters, we could have an annual coon hunter's contest. Billy Bob groaned, no Trace I don't think that would hardly be what I am looking for. Ok Paw, but I will keep thinking, you know how I am about this kind of thing I just keep on thinking.

The next day Trace was back. What you got today Trace said his Father. Well I been thinking more, maybe we could make this a fancy horse, paw. We could have horse judging shows, horse races and just all kind of horse attractions. Billy Bob thought for a whole five minutes on this, one surprised at Trace. Well Trace, I must admit it is a lot better than the first suggestion, but I still don't think it is the right one, sorry. Ok I will keep on thinking until I get one for you that will work.

The next morning Billy Bob hears a loud rap on his door, come on in Trace and tell me what you have today. Trace comes in the door all out of breath, I got it Paw I got it. What is it Trace? Well we can become the "Town Of The Irish Southerners". Here's what we can do, we can have Irish fights with money prizes, won't that be great. They are all beer drinkers, so we can build pubs, and dance halls. The Irish are all lovers so that will be good for a couple of motels. The Irish are big eaters and we should be able to get four maybe five eating houses out of that, just look at the money the town will make. Billy Bob's eyes were big as silver dollars and the thought of money had really set him off.

Billy Bob was all engrossed in the idea and had not spoken a single word in the last fifteen minutes. What about it Paw Trace ask bringing Billy Bob back to the present. I don't know Trace come by in the morning and I will tell you what I think. Trace left happy because he just knew this was it, he had finally made it big, or at least he was going to be big, because he was going to help his Father set this up and just look at the money they would make.

The next morning Trace was waiting at the office when Billy Bob got there. Setting down Trace asked the magic question. Billy Bob frowned, this was going to hurt him. Trace I just don't think it is the right thing to do. As I thought about it last night, about all the Irish people I know I realized that the Irish have been here in America so long that they have become so mixed with other nationalities that the Irish bloodline has become so diluted they will probably not have much interest in some place starting a town affiliation and logo after them, we just can't take the chance. I don't know what you are talking about Paw, but I guess you are right.

Well what about sorghum cooking? Won't work. What about hog killing? Won't work. What about corn cob festival? Hold it right there, eye doggies I believe you might have something there, let me think about it for a couple of days and I will let you know. Trace left all worked up he could just see himself helping his Dad and making money of his own for a change. He was twenty eight years old now and it was time for him to start makings his own money.

Monday morning Trace was up early to see what his Dad had in mind. But Billy Bob was already gone. So Trace put on clean clothes and headed for City Hall. On the way to the office Trace was compiling a list of things to say to his Father, but as he came through the door Billy Bob was already talking. Here is what we are going to do Trace. We are going to have pictures made with adds beneath them and post at all four entrances to town, we are going to have huge corn cobs painted on all empty walls that can be seen from the road, then it will be mandatory for all businesses to have a corn cob on their public entrance doors.

For activities we will have a cob walk beginning behind the bank going all the way to the Senior Citizens building around the back and again ending behind the Bank. All the girls will select a corn cob from a bag and what ever young man's name is on it is who she will walk with. While walking around the Senior Citizens building they will have time to kiss and just might get a romance started. Yea Paw a romance. They might get married said Billy Bob, and remain beholden to us for years.

We will have a corn cob cook off making corn cob relish and corn cob preserves. Now Trace you will be in charge of the preserves cook off so do you think you can be sure that all the stuff is off of the cobs where they will be clean enough to use? Oh yes Paw. Good now I will put Bobby Joe in charge of the relish and that will be taken care of. We have enough wives in town to do the cooking and the men will do the thinking, men make the best managers you know. Trace said nothing.

We will have a rope pull and for everyone with the nerve there will be a jump off. I don't think we will have to set up anything for those sixty-five and older they will be happy just looking on. Food Trace Richard there will be mountains of food.

We will have hot dogs, corn cob hot dogs, hamburgers, corn cob hamburgers and a special Billy Bob hamburger, ribs along with all kind of taters, onions, cucumbers, fried squash, pies ,corn cob cake, tea, water and if we must cokes. People will be begging to breath with their bellies so full. Billy Bob was drooling at the mouth, Money, money, money!!

Can you imagine Trace, we will be rich! Yes Poppa, Yes rich! Watch closely Trace we are going to have new motels, new restaurants, new supermarkets, maybe a new super Wal-mart and two new Banks. Can you see it Trace, can you see it. Trace was jumping up and down with his fist tightly clenched yelling Yes Poppa Bob, Yes I see it, I see it.

Well the Corn Cob Festival got kicked off and did alright, but not with the vigor that Billy Bob had in mind. We still got the signs at the towns entrances, a new restaurant and we have had a singing or two enough to bring in an extra sixty-five dollars tax money. Billy Bob is still looking if you have any suggestions, City Hall.

Chapter Fifteen
Humble Countenance

Vehicles

In the local newspaper we read the article about the County beginning vehicle registration in July. Bubba Joe said, why July? We knew we were in for it having to come up with that much extra money a year. Why its likely to break some of our most needy citizens, said Billy Bob (the mayor).

Billy Bob said that we might just have to go back to horse and buggies and become Mennonites. Mennonites are a group of people that came over from Germany, I think. They had their own way of doing things sort of like the southerners use to, but they never had a civil war. They also didn't have a bunch of Celts that came over from the Celtic country that now are called Yankees.

Any way Billy Bob almost went crazy trying to find a way to help his people without having to dig into his own pocket or the people having to go back to horse drawn vehicles. Finally he called a town meeting and ask for suggestions and this indicated to the whole town that Billy Bob was at last very serious and desperate. Billy Bob swallowed more pride in asking the whole town for suggestions than and old cow does grass in fine hay field. But the people had no real suggestions.

Bubba Joe ask if it might possibly do any good if everyone would act dumb and take tractors, wagons, buggies and hay bailers to be registered, but no one wanted to go along with that. So in final desperation they decided to just go along with it for the first year and see how things went. Well, they were surprised when they found out that the were just taxing a per-cent rate instead of five hundred per vehicle.

Fast Food

Southerners were a little skittish when they started adding fast food to their market. A constant murmur attacked the Snack Shop for the first couple of months. Bubba Joe was very active in the stirring of this new concoction. He approached every one with a few small questions asking what they thought about these new fast food places. The murmurs grew louder and more intense as time progressed but the culprits didn't go away. Bubba Joe grew angrier and angrier with no results and we were afraid he was going to have a heart attack or a stroke until finally his wife threw in the towel. She vowed to Bubba Joe if he didn't stop his attack on the new fast food places, that she was sure as rain water going to go home and live with her Father and Mother.

Bubba Joe's anger finally subsided enough for him to think straight and he admitted that he might have over reacted a little. He never really ever gave in completely because every once in a while you would hear him say; "them places are killing our young people, with all that junky excuses for food they are serving." His wife would give him a hard look and Bubba would just breathe out a long sigh and hush.

Children Did What They Were Told

Down South people are pretty consistent with their neighbors. Most everyone practices the same rules as their resident partners next door, this way they can compare their actions and decisions without conflict. Since one of the southern practices is to learn to live without conflict everyone tries to vote for the same officials for county and local offices. and raise their children the same. These being the two most common friction causing actions the world over, hence the two chosen for the South's most important issues.

These issues are dealt with using the greatest finesse. Communication is top priority as a result and more phone calls are made about the two subjects than any other. Cell phones were not permitted in the South until these issues were voted in as priority items. They decided that the South could put up with the increase in the divorce rate and the doubling of women with a second lovers in order to reduce family feuds.

Then they decided to diversify, meddle as the Yankees call it. School teachers started sending letters home with the children to inform the parents of better ways in instructing their children. Of course this was strictly out of care of the children even though some accused them of trying to become public figures. It continued this way for a long time until parents finally got a belly full and told the teachers to "butt out".

The parents kept "butting in" until the children's "butts" got so sore that they finally decided it was easier to do what their parents told them. This action has saved the South more money than you could ever expect and maybe even a few lives. On top of that we did things our way.

We have saved money on doctor bills through less drunken accidents, we have saved the businessman money through less drunken thievery, and we have also saved the insurance companies money by having less pay outs. It is not good that we have cost the school system more. They have had to put extra money into more janitors, more children at school the greater need for janitors.

The parents like this a lot better however, with all of the children in school the more time they have to put into their businesses and everyone else's. They also have more time for those who have regular jobs to get a little overtime and free time. Making a little extra money a week they can cut out cooking. Isn't that great? Now men can work longer hours and some even enough to afford to hire their lawns mowed. This will allow enough extra time to go to the exercise studio at the tune of thirty dollars a week.

The women are making twenty to twenty-five extra dollars a week allowing them to go to the fast food stores and bring home supper at the tune of thirty-five a week plus. We know it is junk food and not good for them, but maybe it won't hurt them too bad. They now drink cokes and mellow yellow, because they simply don't have the time to make tea in their fast pace. It saves an extra fifteen minutes, almost time enough to swing by Wal-Marts on the way home from work, makes sense don't it?

Now the man of the house, he is making enough extra money to be able to swing by Little Generals and pick up a twelve pack of beer. This will help him to relax a little at night and he sure needs it working an extra hour or two a day, poor fellow. He sure is proud of his children for fixing it where he can relax at night. He is profiting at night at the expense of his children, but the kids don't get any benefit from the extra money he is making. At least he is raising them in accordance to Southern tradition!

The man of the house who doesn't drink? I'm sorry to have been unfair to them. They do not bring in a twelve pack of beer, not at all. They save their money until the weekend and buy it up in lottery tickets thanks to our State Government. I mean after all they just might win some money on one of those tickets and buy their son or daughter a new pair of shoes, goodness knows they need them. If they don't hit it at least they tried.

They are raising their children right aren't they?

Teaching Children To Drive

I once heard that when you get ready to teach your children to drive the best thing to do was to buy you and old beat up car about a three hundred dollar value. The informer said, that in the long run it would save you a lot of money. I knew it was a chore to teach a youngster to drive, but I didn't know it was that bad.

All you can hear the year before they are old enough to teach is, "Mama I want to learn to drive," You almost go nuts during that year and at times come close to giving in to you instantaneous desires. You threaten to run them away from home and when you find out you can't do that you then threaten to kill them. You threaten them with numerous things, but after your threatening to kill them and they live through it they know they got you hooked. Just before it is time to take them on the road the first time you are so crazy you give up, you tell the Lord that you are no longer responsible for your actions and a wild look comes over your countenance.

The last short time you realize that you are totally crazy, your child is totally infuriated at you. You realize that God is all you have on your side, you have talked to God a lot that year and several times just before you wrapped your hands in her hair for the kill God reaches down and strengthens you for a little longer.

Then finally the time has come and little do you know that the last year has really been an easy one. Now comes the real test and God smiles. Lord have mercy.

You prepare yourself for the task ahead, you talk to God one last time. Then with all the nerve you can muster you step out into the unknown. You haven't thoroughly realized yet that you have just taken your and your daughter's life into your hands.

Jumping into the car you drive around the block a couple of times and show each move that she needs to make and she says' "I know." You swallow hard muster a smile and put her under the wheel and if you had any idea what your car was going to look like an hour from now you would never do such a thing, even if she had to walk for the rest of her life.

Then far away you hear something that almost resembles your voice squeak, "put it into drive." She grabs the gear shift and wrenches it downward. You hear, "varoom" and off to the rear you go, "wham." First you thank God for your lives, then you grab her by her hair shake her real good then letting her go you calm yourself. Throwing out the rest of her hair you calmly say again, "put the car into drive."

The next two months are pure agony for Mama. Everything she tries teaching Michelle her daughter would just say, "I know." By the end of that two months Mama's car was so scratched it looked like it had been driven through a field full of Indonesian tigers. Mama was a very unhappy camper to say the least and when she found out that Michelle had eaten a candy bar and wiped the chocolate off her hands on the sides of the seat she went airborne. It looks like someone has been changing baby diapers in here Michelle, what were you thinking.

Mama vows that before the rest of her children are ready to train she is going to buy her a nineteen fifty -five model Chevrolet, one of those handicap models. She maintains that maybe then they will learn to really drive, but might learn to respect other peoples property as well. Mama might just have a good idea there, you know. She also shares that it is wonderful that she doesn't have but three children to teach to drive. More would force her to spend the money for drivers training school.

Give Your Children Less Money

Did you know that Southerners give their children less money than the Yankees. There are a couple or reasons for that and one is that they don't have it or say they don't have it. People from the South are bad about hiding their money, they always have more than they say they do. Some like Billy Bob (our mayor) are pretty thrifty in getting a substantial sum of yours,

They put their money in the funniest places in order to keep it hid. They put it into trust companies, insurance companies, food companies, oil companies and into pharmaceuticals. It appears that they put their money into all the places that they gripe about overcharging them. I don't think any of them are dumb enough to put into the government.

Another reason is that it helps to keep their children out of trouble. If they don't have it then they can't give it to them and the best way is to invest directly from the pay check. It is a proven fact that the children with less money get into less trouble. It is a stair step affair, or as the government calls it, trickle down affair. The more money they have the more beer they can buy, then the more nerve they get, the less eyesight they got, the less brain they got and then they lose all contact with common sense.

Do you know how many of southern kids drink beer, 100%. Do you know how many southern kids get into trouble, 100%. Do you know how many southern kids work, the last account 2.

So we have a small problem, but things are looking up they are expecting a one per-cent increase this year!

The South Teaches Their Children To Work Some Of Them Anyway

When southern children are six years old it is time to start teaching them how to work. The very first of their jobs may be to sweep the front porch or to pick up over the yard. Most all the people of the south think it is a good idea, a few don't think it a good idea and there a those who think it is a good idea but won't do it. These people are the ones who throw a monkey wrench into the work young plan. The rest of us are contemplating running the trouble makers off.

We are sure about one thing, the young who have never had to do anything but lay around all their lives are the ones we will have to maintain welfare for. We will have to be sure to keep some kind of mother's benefits for those who don't know how to do anything but breed.

We researched welfare people and came up with a few things concrete. If grownups are lazy and good for nothing but to lay up on their backsides with no ambition, then their children are going to follow in their footsteps. If parents get up in the morning and go off looking for some new approach to get a new check started from the government instead of looking for a job. How do you think their children are going to act? If a parent of a fatherless home keeps increasing the size of her family to increase the size of her check. What do you think her children are going to do? So when you find out that your children won't work, it might be a good idea to check out your background before you go to blaming it on the child!

Now let us look at a different angle. Suppose a no good husband and father abandons his wife and family and will not send any money home to support his family, do you think the mother has a legitimate right to search for help. Of course she does, but her chances of getting enough help to go to the trouble are slim, very slim. It seems that our government offices that control these benefits give it to the lazy, I have a headaches, and make it hard on the ones that really need it. It is a shame that the controlling individuals act like they are the ones providing the money for these programs. I will bet the government does not review these programs and their employees twice a year and it should be done every quarter.

So hear ye all you young lazy chemical cookers, if you are able to work and know how to amble convincingly with a walking stick, just run on down to your nearest Human Services Office and pick up your check. However if you are surviving on water gravy three times a day, only have one child who has no medical service to get him over infantigo, measles and inflated stomach from lack of vitamins, you can forget it, unless you get the right Congressman behind you.

Hooray for our fluidly operating Human Services Department.

Chapter Sixteen
The Big Cook Off

It was a cool crisp morning in September of 1948 when we left the house to catch the horses for their day's work, and ours of course. I was six and one half years old and ready to get started with the plans for the day. Full of sausage, eggs and pancakes that were giving me more energy than I needed I was itching to see my Father harness the horses and connect to the sorghum press. Today we were going to begin the sorghum cook off that always began this time of the year, man was I excited.

Bubba Joe continues on with the story, he probably hasn't told it over three hundred times. Bubba has a way of hanging onto the past and balling it all up into a story, so hang on!

I could hardly wait because when the sorghum juice begins to run into the cooking pan it produced foam in the cooking that most all youngsters were crazy about. We ate it until it tore our stomachs all to pieces and we would throw up and run to the outhouse for the next forty-eight hours. As youngsters we didn't mind so badly, it only happened once a year.

We watched the sorghum fields for the last month waiting for it to ripen and cure reaching the right stage to cut, pressed and cooked into molasses. Ah! The rich sweetness of the sorghum juice was always cooked into a thick molasses that graced the tables of most southern homes. Its distinct rich flavor was the perfect addition to the south's family table. Good and good for you was Mom's description of the grand food. Blessed by God, prepared by the Father, served by the Mother and enjoyed by the entire family.

For the families that made or had sorghum molasses made by a neighboring farmer was always proof that you were loved. For the rest it was always blackberry or strawberry preserves. What a wonderful life we had growing up, if children today witness a few of these experiences it would most probably change their lives.

So while the light slowly crept into existence the team was harnessed and the plan was set into action. My Father knew exactly what to do and everything went like clockwork. Two of the neighbors that were having their sorghum cooked off here were in the field cutting and stacking the sorghum cane. My Father's brother that was living with us had taken one of the horses my Father had harnessed and led it to the press. He hooked the horse to the long curved handle or press pole that hung above the horse's head. The handle was connected to the horse's collar, which was part of his harness and always looked like some huge funny monster. Late in the afternoon when the shadows began to crawl the press pole became a bit scary looking in the shadows.

Then came the first load of sorghum cane to the press on a flat bed trailer, cut into exact lengths and ready for the press. My Father had already built the fire under the cooking pan and after the fire reached a certain temperature, which my Father seemed to know by heart or by just looking at it, he would then signal the man operating the press. Uncle Warner clicked at the horse and as the horse began to move the press was put into motion and the cooking stage began. By nightfall many a half gallon bucket would be full of the sweet nectar, to be placed in storage for winter use. It almost appeared to be a miracle to us youngsters.

Creak, squeak, chatter chatter the old mill press continued its never-ending song. As the two large steel drums rolled side by side squeezing the juice from the cane it ran down into a small wood lined bucket into a trough that ran down the hill some thirty to fifty feet and into the cooking pan. The cooking pan was separated into several long narrow compartments, which allowed the juices to move slower through the cooker.

Soon the bubbles would begin to jump and pop as the juices reached the boiling point. As it grew hotter and boiled faster the foam began to rise on top of the partially cooked syrup, along with our excitement. This is exactly what the six happy young people had been patiently waiting for and their taste buds were near the bursting point. Sometime you could find more foam at the corner of their mouths than on the cooking syrup.

It appeared that Mother had known exactly when the foam would rise, because she appeared at the cooking pan with a bowl of biscuits that she had made extra at breakfast time and six bowls. My Mother was a darling lady and never missed having everything ready for us children at every special occasion that happened throughout the year.

With our bellies full of sorghum foam and biscuits we laid back in the shade until my Dad would call for more heating wood. We never really wanted to bring any wood to the cooker, because we were too busy getting sick enough to throw up, but we knew better than to complain for Dad had been patient with us while we were waiting for the foam and then having our feast. So we trudged to the woodpile and brought back enough wood to fire the cooker. It would last for a little while so it was back to the shade and Dad would hide his grin and say; " thank you boys".

Things really begin to get serious then, Dad would find us more work to do as we got sicker at our stomachs. We got to help load the wagon in the field and the jarring and bumping didn't help anything, but they were nice enough to stop and let us throw up and then back to work. Another would get to help feed the press with sorghum cane. Of course bending didn't help the sickness any. It really was not the bending that was bad but the straightening up.

So we would run to the side and throw up and then back to the press, we got behind a little of course, but nothing was said. The lucky one got to stay with the cooker and help my Dad. If you were not already sick you would get that way here. The smell of the hot cooking sorghum will drive you insane if you are sick already on sorghum foam. You almost cannot hold it long enough to get far enough away from the cooker not to contaminate what is cooking in the pan.

By nightfall you are sick as a dog, worn out completely and hate the very thought of cooking off sorghum, but tomorrow is another day and you will have to be prepared to face it.

All in all it was a pretty exciting two days except for the fact that during the night your sickness took a turn for the worse. It turned from the north and headed south at break neck speed. So the second day you are running to the privy all day.

However as the days go by you forget about the bad happenings and remember the good ones. By next years season you will be as excited as you were yesterday. And you just can't wait until next years Big Cook Off comes around .

CHAPTER SEVENTEEN
Preparing Hogs For Winters Food

The Preparation And The Killing Time

In the spring there is a certain things that takes place that will be with all young Southerners. The greening of their private worlds, the warming of the Master Global atmosphere. Bubba Joe says, "man you talk about rising adrenalin, you can catch it by the gallons." He said, "the finding of the first warm pond can do wonders for the imagination."

Then of course you start getting them hogs ready for the killing. You must feed them regularly. They like corn and a mixture in the olds days called slop. Most every farmer kept from one to four five gallon buckets on the back porch for slop. His wife would put the left over eggs, sausage, gravy and sorghum molasses from breakfast in then first. When she finished washing up her dishes in her dishpan, then she would pour her wash water in there too. Billy Bob said, that sometimes it smelled pretty good until she poured in the wash water. You would have to pour water on the ground in different places so the hogs would have a place to wallow in the mud, and according to Bubba Joe to keep cool.

After this came the castrating the young males. Alford always let his hogs get too big before castrating, as did most farmers. His reasoning for this was to be able to pick out the one to keep for breeding. He reasoned that the biggest one would produce the best piglets. He knew that he would need more and bigger boys for the castration, but determined it was worth it. Of course some of the farmers just forgot it was that time again,

So the boys were called in on that special day at Alford Joe's pig castration day. They were to catch the pig and throw him on the ground. One boy was to straddle the pig and hold his back legs, the next boy was to hold his front legs and set on his head while the farmer cut away the extra things that weren't needed. You never heard so much squealing and noise in your life. Some boys just were not tough enough to watch what happened.

Alford said he sure hated to put them boys through that experience, but who is going to do the killing when we are gone. These boys need the experience from somewhere while they are young so I guess it was my calling.

The time has finally come to kill the hogs, not many showed up. According to our hog expert Alford Joe, first they had to be shot and between the eyes was the best place. It was then someone's job to rush in and cut the hogs throat so as much of his blood could escape as possible. Immediately he was put into a large vat of boiling water and all his hair scraped off him. The poor hog was at this time hung up by his back feet and his stomach ripped open to extract his entrails. After washing out the inside he was then cut up into sections to be hung up and cured.

After being cured during the winter he was cut up into cooking size and really made for some good eating while the snows were on the ground.

Sausage, bacon and tenderloin really made a winter breakfast topped off with butter, biscuits and sorghum molasses along with hot coffee. Shoulders and hams were good for dinner and supper and an occasional breakfast meat. What better could you ask for?

We are not done yet. All the extra pieces left over from the hog including fat were cooked off into lard. All these parts were put into a huge black iron kettle and a fire built under it to cook the grease out of the fat pieces and after it reached a boiling temperature it was cooled and used for lard to cook with, just like cooking oil is today, remember. Alford Joe says, he sure hopes you have enjoyed this trip back to our younger days and hog killing time.

CHAPTER EIGHTEEN

Creations From The South

Christmas Presents

In Southern England and Holland where most of us so called rebels come from. Years ago the were having a severe problem in rearing their children so they got together to try finding something that would that would improve the morale of their children. As everywhere the Englanders and Hollanders had some children that were cry babies. It was horrible, they could not find a way of soothing these kids. In their search to address this issue a southern Englishman who was a shop maker came up with the idea to give them presents once a year. Later after long discussion they finally put a date on it, December 12th. It has been changed many times through the years, but I guess they have finally came to a conclusion.

With good cause they decided to give the presents in December, because they had the whole winter ahead and the children would spend most of the winter inside. Since Christopher Yearlin was the one to come up with the idea they decided to name the day after him, hence Christmas.

Now at this time in history there was never any money to buy presents for anyone so an alternative method was needed.

They bargained with a dozen carpenters the first year to make the presents needed to hold the first Christmas day. It worked great mechanically, but it broke their reserves for other necessities. So it was then decided that each head of the household after taxes would provide their own gifts for the family. Apples and oranges were reasonably cheap in England at that times so needless to say for most this was what they got for Christmas.

Since Holland was famous for their flowers they decided to give them to their children for presents. This worked fine for a couple of years until a young Hollander got hold of his father's gun and shot him. When ask why he had shot his father he said; "I just got tired of having nothing but tulips in my stocking." This created the need for something more fashionable for the season and finally a man in Southern America created a pair of shoes from a 2x4 and Holland immediately began to import from America to solve the problem. So the South came through three times for the world from this one simple little problem. No more cry babies, presents to give at Christmas time and shoes to protect the feet of the world.

Swimming Pools

In the earlier South after people learned that humans could swim, they were restricted to swimming in rivers and ponds. This created a little problem of having to take a bath after going in at the river or pond. Then another problem arose. The only thing they had to swim in was men's overalls and women's night gowns. This swim wear was very annoying, because men got their overall straps hung on limbs and the women had to stay away from the bushes along the banks, something simply must be done.

They had Saturday night barbeques and Sunday dinners trying to figure out what could be done. They finally decided that it would be acceptable for men to cut the legs off their overalls to the knee and women could cut off the night gowns to the knee if they would sew it up the middle up to the critical area. For years this worked wonderful until some guy got dollar bills in his eyes and made swim suits that came up to the critical area for both men and women. They were then renamed bathing suites so they could be called acceptable.

After the creation of swim suits they had to come up with some way to get the mud out of the water and critical areas. This became a world affair and the challenge was accepted in all countries. Nothing seemed to work until one engineer from Pascagoula, Alabama a Walter Ben Hidgett got in on the hunt, and he promised to have a working model within one year.

Walter Ben had this large hole in his backyard he had been intending to fill up for two years and he decided to incorporate it into the project. Walter Ben was called WB by most people and one of his neighbors called WB one night and offered to give him a pile of large rock to fill up his hole in the yard and WB knowing he just might could use it in his project accepted. He worked hard for a month lining the hole with these large rock and he was very proud of his work because it turn out to look very nice.

WB thought about the hole every moment he was awake and how rough the floor was. And one night at three o'clock it snap into place. What he would do would be put him a drain in the floor of the hole and pour concrete around the walls and it would hold water. He would call it a swimming pool and put chemicals in it once in a while to keep the water clean. Thanks to WB another creation chalked up to Great Southern Creations.

Electricity

There was an old man somewhere up around the New England states, Virginia, Pennsylvania, Maryland or some place like that who was outside in a thunderstorm playing with a kite and a key tied on the end of it and almost got himself electrocuted. Now I know that sounds childish, but then so many things do.

A relative of Bubba Joe and Alford Joe heard about this silly thing happening and came up with an idea to make power from it. Harold Dean Butcher was their relatives name and Harold Dean had already made an electric drill and saw, but it was unhandy on the job, because it took two men to turn the crank to the dynamo. He was a great inventor however and I got the story first hand from Bubba and Alford Joe.

Harold Dean told his wife that night that he had been thinking it over and that he was going to make electric power from the old man's kite and key foolishness. His wife told him that she had never heard of anything so stupid in her entire life. Instantly Harold Dean knew he had a winner and he started laying plans.

Harold Dean worked day and night on his project, without food or sleep. He cut, sanded, drilled and put medal together endlessly. In six months he had a model, he could run several lights from his first converter. He was so happy he demonstrated it to everybody, and then one day some government boys showed up and explained how much healthier it would be for everyone if they took over the issue from here, and they took away his converter. Poor Harold was devastated and under so much stress from the loss of his invention, he finally lost so much weight from not being able to eat, he died. Poor man didn't even get his name put on the converter as the inventor. He was stripped of his dignity, no wonder he died.

Anyway the South still knows about how electricity got started and we can chalk up another creation for the South.

CHAPTER NINETEEN
The South Is Gonna Own This Nation

I was talking to Billy Bob (our mayor) yesterday and he informed me that the South was getting tired of how these young whippersnappers in Congress are running this country. He put his hand beside his mouth and whispered the news that there is a movement in the South to take over.

He enlightened me that all the businesses in this country have began to save their monies for this purpose including certain biggies like Wal-Mart, Walgreen and Tom's Food, Ltd. All the States are in on it and all the Governors are already having secret meetings, you know like the group of businessmen that meet in Monaco every year. They say, that if we can pool enough money we can take over. I agreed with him, because Wal-Mart alone could just about do it. Just think about what would happen if Wal-Mart joined forces with Iran, Iraq and Kuwait, scary isn't it.

The last account I had Wal-Mart has about 350 stores here in the US, about 250 stores overseas. I don't know about overseas, but that is near half the business in America since NAFTA. You ally them with Walgreen and Tom's Food Ltd. and you got power.

Then there are a host of other businesses based in the south who can make themselves heard through financial power.

Billy Bob says, his constituents believes that they can change the direction of this country and take over. By leading them correctly he chimes we can stop the war, stop abortion and stop gay movements in the bedroom and bathroom. Then we can start to work on getting some of these idiotic bills rescinded. If we don't get something done soon folks he reiterated by the next presidential election we won't be able to say anything about the government or political aggression.

We put our intellectual hound dog Rafe on the job of collecting information for us and he bragged that they are already putting people in jail in Canada for talking about gays on the street. He said that they are calling it hate speech and they ain't letting no one get away with it either. I ask him if they were putting people in jail for talking about God. No he said, I reckon you can still run God down anywhere and get away with it, but I informed him that they just thought they were getting away with it.

One other thing I have noticed is that can still say anything about women and get away with it. Our women haven't figured out yet that gays have been out a notch or two above, but when they do, walk softly now.

So-si-a-tee. You think the movie "Code Of Silence" was rough, you ain't seen nothing yet. Who has the most class and the most power are big issues among women and they will go to any length to show you. These girls can stir up more ---- in an hour than an army of men can in a month, go girls. And guess what, they are backing us in taking over this country.

I am surprised that Billy Bob backing the women when his wife ran off with a carpenter. He surely must see some money in it for him some where down the line. I haven't got it figured out yet, so we are all still ignorant to his motives.

Our mayor says, "that we are still working on the mechanics of this movement. That when we get it running smoothly we are going to take over this Nation. I reminded him that the South had already had their butt kicked once and maybe they should slow down just a bit. Nah; you see we are working on a new angle this time. We are going to do it like the US and Russia did in the cold war. Please tell me I said!

Well, and he put his hand to the side of his mouth again, we are going to make this a psychological mission, we are gonna work on the Yankee's minds. By the time we get done with them, the Yanks won't know if they are going or coming and whether they are doing it forward or backward.

You see my friend this is gonna be done by brain power. And what is going to make it fool proof is, we have some women on our staff. These are five of the most cold hearted babes you have ever seen. They are five feet tall, thin, cold hungry blondes who can smell money in an outhouse. Ah man; do we have a treat in store for the yanks, yep we gonna own this country.

CHAPTER TWENTY
Do Southern Women Obey Their Husbands

Maybe the real question should be do southern men obey their wives? Men seem to think they are still the head of the house or family and the men that think that way may be just a little bit light upstairs or just trying to fool the rest of the world. Due to our tax laws men are still the head of the household until proven otherwise. Regardless of our men, our taxes and our laws, we have a large number of men who are holding a position and not doing the job.

Women who are wives, mothers and income helpers are the greatest psychologist on earth. They are the most capable people in the world executing mind control and men control. Any one who can control the household, make all the family decisions, handle all the money and make their husbands that he is doing it are truly top psychologist. They are capable of raising their children to be whatever it is she wants them to be without having to kill a single one of them and that's a miracle within itself.

They hold down a full time job just like hubby does and are able to get hubby to feel sorry for them for having so terribly much to do. When the truth is they love having a job, because it's the only stress reducer they have.Not only are there questions about his capabilities on his daytime job, but he falls short on his night time job as well. So their only route to reducing stress is to work. How does a job reduce stress, don't ask me I don't understand either. You should be asking a woman!

Men gloat about the statement that they are the stronger to the sexes, wrong. Men are wimps, thoroughbred total wimps and some might even cry if you tell them that. Let us see if we can paraphrase a little in behalf of the female sex! Honey, would you make me a sandwich? Honey, would you bring me a beer? Honey, would you see you you can stop those two kids from fighting? Honey, are my tan jeans clean I want to wear them tomorrow? All this time he has been laying on the couch watching the ball game and acting like he is just about half dead.

Next we hear honey, it is beddy bye time. What do you mean you're too tired, you haven't done that much today.

Of course he is right all she has done was get up at four o'clock and get breakfast started so her kids and husband can have breakfast before they leave. She has layed out the childrens school clothes and checked their nose and nails to be sure they were clean. Layed out hubby's shorts, socks, tan jeans and shirt so he can get ready for work. She makes sure everyone has been fed and without any food she takes the kids to school on her way to work. At 9am she finally gets a break and has time to choke down a sausage and biscuit for herself.

After a full days work she rushes to the sitter and picks up her children, takes them home and gets them started on their lessons. Then she gets the honors of putting supper on for Mister Macho and the kids. Alternately she puts supper on the stove a load of clothes in the washer and supper cookware in the dishwasher. About this time Mister Macho makes his appearance and wants to know why he doesn't have any tea poured. She pours his tea, finishes with the dishwasher that hubby didn't think she needed until one day he agreed to do the dishes.She then takes the first load out of the washer puts them into the dryer and reloads the washer

Mom finally gets to go to the table and sit down for her unearned supper when little Bobby starts screaming bloody murder. Mister Macho says, go see what is wrong with that kid, and make it snappy while he is still living. Now here is grounds for murder, but Mom just goes to see about Bobby.

After cleaning the table, refilling hubby's tea glass, puts the dirty dishes in the dishwasher, empties the washing machine, folds two loads of clother and puts them away and vacuums the carpet she can sit down and rest a few minutes before hubby yells bedtime.

Any more dumb questions bright guy? Of course I am not tired, of course I haven't done anything today and of course you are as full of four letter bologna as anyone I have ever seen. Now then if you put another hand on me you are going to pull back two nubs, understand. And hubby says, "gosh honey there ain't no need of getting mad about it. I ain't getting mad I am already mad" she screamed.

I have never seen anything as proficient as a woman. She can carry on a full conversation, soothe her five years, pour coffee for the neighbor and throw sexy winks at her husband all at the same time and make it all effective. I can see why God burned up eighty thousand computers trying to make a woman and still wound up having to wing it. But all in all he did a pretty good job. Except for the blondes and the sun is still getting to their brains.

CHAPTER TWENTY ONE
Who Created This Earth

Southerner who participate are a Christian people who read and believe the Bible. The number of church goers in the South are pretty high and I guess that is why we are called the Bible Belt. Yet there are people the world over that are still trying to disprove the Bible and the teachings of God. It is sad that anyone would knowingly throw their life away just to be like celebrities or to appear to be like all the others within a University or an ungodly church.

So the big question is who made the Earth? Really now this should not be hard to figure out. It is written in the Bible in the first book and the first chapter, nothing to it easy to find. Of course if you decide to read and believe it you will be inviting trouble. Satan, the opposition to God, will find one million things to put into your mind to try and change it. Do you remember once you were thinking about doing something that would have been good for a friend or relative and all out of the blue one of the most foul evil things popped into your mind, opposing your intentions. That was Satan. He can fill your mind so full of evil you will wonder about yourself.

Do you remember one day when you had some bad thoughts that you didn't like on your mind and all out of the blue your mind

cleared and you felt peaceful within yourself? T
is that confusing, it is Satan, it is that simple, it i
scary, it is Satan, it is that simple, it is God. Goc
our God the master designer who created this anc
charge of it, regardless of what anyone thinks.

Sometime when you have plenty of time and nothing to do, find a nice quite place where you will not be disturbed and think about the following questions.

1. Who created the Earth- the mountains and the millions of tiny insects, germs and microscopic life forms it takes to maintain the earth?
2. Who created Man- The body, the heart, the mind and all the microscopic life forms it takes to maintain your life, who gave you breath?
3. Who created the Oceans- With millions of life forms that have constantly moved about its floor for six thousand years?
4. Who created Plant Life- Millions of different species that are dependant upon each other?
5. Why is the earth dependant upon water?
6. Why is man dependant upon plant life and water?
7. Why is Aquatic life dependant upon underwater plant life and other underwater life forms?
8. Who is responsible for the bodies of worldly life forms that take in foods process it and excrete it back into the system from whence it came to be reused or recycled?
9. How could man be able to understand all the cycles of life when he can't even cure cancer?
10. Why can't man understand that God put us here to be dependant upon each others resources and live in harmony instead of trying to kill each other?
11. Why is it that man no longer wants God to tell him what to do?

. Why is it that man thinks he is now smarter than God, that he can take care of himself and by himself?

13. Why is it that man will put his mind, his heart and his body up for sale for the sake of worldly materials?

14. Why did God create this earth and all that is within it?

I realize that answering these fourteen questions without God will be impossible, but it will give you a place to start in believing. These questions also create a scary scenario of earth becoming a killing place for warmongers and people who would control this earth without any kind of love and compassion for his fellowman.

All hope is not gone, with God it can still be a place of peace and joy. It can be a place of compassion between brothers of Christ. It can be a place of happiness without war between nation and men. It can be a place of teaching and growing in God's word.

God gave us instructions how to do this, had it put into book form for easy use and promised to teach us what we needed to know. All this and the only restrictions put upon it was that we must believe in Him, accept Him, and live accordingly.

Have you ever considered that even if there was no God, the Bible would still make more sense than men ever have. But there is a God and the time will come when all men will know. Every Knee will bow and every tongue will confess.

One more time now; Who Made This Here Earth? Read John 3-16, Revelation chapters 21 and 22 every day for the next thirty days, then come back and answer the 14th questions.

CHAPTER TWENTY TWO
What's Normal In The South

People all over the Nation have been trying to figure the answer to that question for a great number of years and failed. So rather than to labor at explaining it to the world when I am not sure myself, maybe I had better just tell you what is not normal in the South. Perhaps I might add that what isn't normal here the people are very eager to tell you in no certain or uncertain terms exactly how they feel about the subject.

They are not trying to be offensive and would not offend you at all if you do not bring up certain subjects. However, they do feel if you bring up a subject then you want to know how they feel about it, so be prepared to ride it out.

One thing they do not feel is normal is not being able to speak freely about God. Bubba Joe thinks that if they do not want you to talk about God then why did they include him in the first place. Why was this country founded on the principles of God? Why is the Ten Commandments strowed all over the White House and Washinton D.C. Why are the two words LAUS DEO standing 555 feet 5 inches tall atop the Washington Monument meaning "Praise Be To God" Why were hundreds of churches allowed to pop up all over America. Why were millions of people spurred on in the belief of God by political speeches. Why are lawyers allowed to pursue demeaning acts toward God when the people really don't mean it. So far so good Bubba Joe.

Why are we passing bills which are attached to the bottom of major polical bills passing through both houses that are taking away certain inalienable rights. Such as, taking prayer and anything else they can get passed out of schools and away from our country's youth, teaching them to disbelieve the Bible before they can read it. Why are certain officials entertaining the thought of taking away the right to pray in Jesus name.

Why are our young allowed to premeditate the digging up of female bodies for their entertainment and do nothing about it. It is said that nothing can be done because there is no laws in that state against premeditating or digging up bodies. Well it is kind of funny that they can introduce new laws against praying in school but they can't introduce laws against defamation of human bodies, strange!

Why are young and certain others getting away with murder in our country? Why are aliens coming here from other countries and getting laws changed that have been in effect since the dawn of our Nation? Why are new laws about money being passed every few months and making it hard for our young to get a start in life? Why is it that if you have ever been in a little trouble as a young person you can not get a credit card or have a bank account? And why every one is judged by the credit score? It makes it appear that our grown-ups are not as grown up as society says they are.

It gives an aura of red light over our country, the country that use to be the leading Nation of the world kind of leaves a bitter taste in your mouth. It is why the rest of the world is not holding us as high as they once did and we are headed downward at the speed of light. It is because of the people and the government and the desire for money more money.

Look at the business attitude of the nation, take what the other person has with no remorse. Send our factories overseas and leave America jobless. Give a three per-cent pay raise and raise product and utility prices ten per-cent. Do you remember what other countries have operated with that attitude before the fell? When those countries began worrying about how they looked to the rest of the world instead of how they actually were, then bad things began to happen. That is exactly the way it was predicted to happen in the Bible thousands of years ago.

Have we progressed after accepting these new attitudes? Anyone can plainly see that we haven't and we can't blame that on some other party because we have all had a hand in it. And if it wasn't because of something that you did, then it was because of something that you didn't do. No matter how big you are, how important you are or how powerful you are you can not escape the wrath of God. Man is just not that intelligent yet, nor will he ever be.

Oh, I understand that man does not like God telling him what to do. I also understand that man thinks he is now smarter than God and that he can handle things on his own so he is just going to push God aside and do it himself. The further he pushes God away the worse shape this country gets in and will some day finally destroy his own country. It is a shame than man can see no further ahead than they are at this point in time. It just ain't normal.

I have heard the story that there are several military training camps occupied by other countries right here in America and nothing is being done about it because they are MAAS, MOS or something and can't be asked to leave. If our government would do what they should they would tell them that if they were going to live here they would have to liquidate these camps. That if they wanted to train everyday in whay resembles military camps they would have to go back to the country where they came from.

Now this is what my friend Bubba Joe had to say about it and as amatter of fact he had a lot more than that to say about it, but that was the only things that were decent enough to put into print. Alford Joe agreed with him with the addition that the government was taking away our rights a little at a time with each new bill introduced into and passed by congress.

Billy Bob our mayor, gets very angry with our government, not pleased with them at all and he is making a killing under the present parliament. He says however that under the new democrat congress he is going to make more than he ever has, can you imagine?

Even the women, who aren't allowed to say much about the government, are beginning to become very upset and a constant roar is being heard from their department. You know how it is when women get stirred up. They have more ba nerve than the men do and they go after what they want full force. If you know about this movement that is almost certain to gain speed shortly then you better change your ways, because women no compassion on men or women with wrong headed ideas.

So I suggest that it may be time to start getting things back to the way they were in the latter 1960's. It may be time to start asking the opinions of the female populace, just to be on the safe side. You men have no idea what real destruction is, just wait until the women take over the war department. And because they are stimulated by the few macho men we have, they will most likely put the majority of the pot bellied men into war camps with personal trainers and trim some of their bellies down to where the belt buckle can be seen. This may be the last warning!

Chapter Twenty Three

Wal-Mart Communities

I don't know if you have ever given any thought to the possibilities of Wal-Mart power. It can be very scary thinking about this major business power. Well one of my friends and I were discussing this once a very short time ago and he awakened me to some possibilities that litterally scaried my socks off me, bet you thought I was going to say pants.

Bobby Joe Harris told me that the day was coming when Wal-Mart would almost completely control the residential world. He says that one day soon we would hear about a new Wal-Mart store being built that was five times bigger than the average Mall. Now that's a biggy, and that you would be able to buy anything you needed or wanted to buy there. That would be good for rainy winter days all under one roof. The new name will be Wal-Mart Gigantic Super Center Mall, a little long but covers it all.

Furthermore he says that they would buy the adjoining ten thousand acres to their Mall and build apartments on it. Whites and Blacks will have first choice at the best apartments, then the Mexicans and Hispanics will be next and last the Middle East Imports. Whites and Blacks will pay 400.00 per month, Mexicans and Hispanics will pay 300.00 per month and the Middle East

Imports will live there free and the government will send them a check for 1500.00 per month to live on.

Bobby Joe Harris you are joking with me aren't you? No he said, and that ain't all the first four groups will have to work in the nearby chicken factories, pig factories, and cow factories making food for America to eat and using the left overs if there is any to make pet food. One proud pig factory in Allendoria Mississippi braggs that they use everything but the squeal and they sell that to toys-n-us.

Bobby Joe told me a whole lot more about Wal-Mart, but I can't go any further, because I am afraid I might get some of you too upset. I wouldn't want to do that with it getting so close to Thanksgiving and all, I will tell you later.

I heard about an engineering company that has come up with a new type apartment complex. Ever third and fourth apartment are connected at the back entrance by a extra long deck for the benefit of families that want to live together. I would not be surprised if Wal-Mart did not buy their plans to use in The Wal-Mart Communities.

Wal-Mart Communities will be a lot different that regular apartment complexes. In an adjoining town there was a new apartment complex built this year. You drive into the complex and drive a quarter of a mile at least then you make a long u-turn and come back up the other side. There were to be one hundred eleven apartments in this complex and they have about three quarters of them completed.

Wal-Mart Communities will not be built on a u-turn drive they will be built on sort of a snake drive to break the monotony. You know how it is people get tired of looking straight up the street and seeing the same ole houses all the time.

Wal-Mart says that they are not going to allow any more than one family to an apartment and with no more than three children. They said they were no going to allow any more than two cars families live there. They are considering allowing the third car to stay overnight on Saturday night, but not for sure yet.

They are not going to allow any pets at all except for the middle east imports and they can have dogs and cats both. I hear in some countries they eat dogs and cats, is that true. I sure am glad we never started eating them down south here. I am afraid I would just have to refuse, I don't think I could stand that.

In the rumor I heard they told that some of the housing projects that Wal-Mart will establish will be mobile home parks. Most of them will be single wide. There will be about ten per-cent of the trailers that will be double wide for the express purpose of the middle east imports. The biggest problem will be tieing them down, but Wal-Mart ran a survey and decided that the best way to tie down is to go over the mobile home with two or three straps like they did when they first started selling them. Wal-Mart decided they had rather for the trailers to be a little uglier than to have their investment blown away.

I ask Bobby Joe Harris if he was planning on living in one of those communities and he said ,yes. Me and Bubba Joe both have decided that we might try living there if they fix them up and make them really look nice, what do yo think.

Chapter Twenty Four
Southerner's Vacation

Where in the world are we going this year. We have been everywhere and there is no place else to go. We went to Minnesota one year and got some berries, Florida one year and got some oranges, went to Washington one year and got some apples and last year we went to Maine and got some blueberries, man were they good.

We got to find a new list of places to go, I even made a list of places to go in yankee country and my family made so much fun of me I finally just threw the list away. One of these days when they are not paying any attention I am going to sneak off up north and see what yankee country looks like. I have heard it is pretty country there, but no one in my family will believe it.

People from the South don't care a thing in the world about going to Europe either they say nothing but sissies live over there. I tried to explain to them that they are not sissies in Europe maybe a little different, but then isn't everyone. Bobby Joe said he didn't want to go any place where he couldn't understand the music and when they sing they screamed to the top of their lungs and wiggled their voice.

Bubba Joe said, "Bobby what do you mean wiggly their voice?" Bobby Joe just looks at him and goes uh UH uh UH uh UH, you get the idea Bubba?

Southerners are big fishermen so a lot of their vacations are fishing. Bubba Joe and Bobby Joe got together one fall to go on a little fishing trip. Bubba Joe always kept a boat hid away in a secret place on the Obion river. They would then take a small river up into the swamp off the big river to fish.

So this trip as usual up into the swamp they go intending to catch a mess of fish and be back home in time to have them for supper. First they would have to clean the fish then clean themselves and be ready when the fish were done.

Their wives were to have all the side dressings ready in time to fry the fish for the supper meal. Bobby Joe said to Bubba,

"man I can almost taste them fish already. We got to be sure to fillet them so we won't have to be too particular when we eat them. Can't you smellum cooking already, Bubba?"

It is always a treat to sit down at the table full of golden brown fillets along with hush puppies, white beans, relish and coleslaw and all the ice tea you can drink to flush'em down with. The boys had been thinking about that all the way to the little river. So they had no idea what was about to happen to them!

They shoved their boat into the water on the big river and made it just fine up to the big river. Here they always took the boat out of the water and carries it across a little box woods and put it in the water on the little river to fish. This way they would not have to paddle upstream. When the fishing trip was over they would float down to the big river on the way home.

They crossed the box woods, but as they arrived at the little river they noticed that the rain the night before had made the little river very swift. Very unhappy about the swift water they still decided they would fish hoping maybe by the time to go home that the water would have slowed considerably. So they put in at their favorite place.

Their plans were to cross the river to a favorite little cove under some overhanging branches. Here they always had good luck catching prize fish and their catch was always a lot quicker. So in goes the boat, the push off and they were on the way across the river with big rewards on their mind.

Halfway across they began to lose the battle with the currents. The boat turned and started down stream and as hard as they tried they could not turn the boat again to finish crossing.

Down the river they go at break neck speed for a quarter of a mile with Bobby Joe hollering to the top of his lungs turn---turn boat----turn----turn you danged boat.

All of a sudden the boat slowed and turned across stream. Another swift wave hit the side of the boat turning it over. Both were dumped into the swift cold water and Bubba grabs and extended branch on the slower side, but Bobby Joe is taken downstream ahead of the boat. What happened next scared Bobby seriously. A wave of cold water and the boat came right over the top of Bobby and out of sight. The force of the water pushed him upon top of a huge limb and would not let him out of the swift current.

Bubba by the might of his own strength had gotten out of the water and onto the bank. He yells over to Bobby Joe, "you alright Bobby Joe?" Yes I'm okay, says Bobby. "Then I am going down to the big river and save the boat, be back after you shortly. Okay says Bobby meekly, but please hurry.

Bobby Joe said to his partner on the way home, "man this was the worst vacation I have ever been on.

Later Bubba was ask why he went after the boat first, "well that's the best boat I've ever owned."

Bubba's wife Helen Sue and her friend Ella Mae Pfleuger went on a cruise once. They finally talked their husbands into letting them go and they were really in a big way about going on a cruise. Out of one hundred sixty two million Southerners they were the fourth and fifth ones to ever go on a cruise. Helen Sue had not smiled in two months, but after finding out that her vacation was a sure thing, she had been smiling for two months.

Bubba Joe said, "she was smiling all over, you know we might just get another baby boy out of this."

They went to Florida and boarded their cruise ship and were off on their seven day cruise. Both ladies were keyed to the hilt and Ella Mae said to Helen out of the blue, "you know it really don't feel right going off without our men. Yeah Helen Sue responded, but we'll get use to it."

All went well the first four days and they were having a wonderful time. They were eating high on the hog, dancing watching the dolphins play and making new friends

Now I must say that Helen Sue Pierce is a very beautiful woman, but up until the cruise no one had ever made a pass at her and if you could see Bubba Joe you would know why. One darkly tanned Latin gentleman had been watching her closely and didn't know Bubba. Helen Sue had seen him watching her, but had not become worried about it. After all he was a handsome gentleman and Helen Sue was kind of flattered by it.

She left her friend and went to her compartment to change her blouse one afternoon she had dropped some soda pop on. Upon sliding her key into the lock on her door she couldn't get it to open. Out of nowhere came her handsome Latin gentleman took the key and on first try opened the door and followed her into the room.

He made a bit of small talk and Helen begin to like him, he reminded her so much of Bubba Joe. She was instantly aware of how much she missed Bubba Joe and a small tear formed in her eyes, Her Latin friend noticed, stepped forward and put his arms around her and said softly, "it will be alright." Helen raised her head to respond to his remark and he kissed her. When their lips met her being off guard she temporarily responded to his kiss. This really turned him on and Helen Sue almost lost control.

Helen sue told her friend later that by the time she came back to her right mind that her Latin was making some music she had never heard before and almost surrendered. It was not easy, but she did manage to get him out of the room without a scene.

Making it back to her friend she told her the whole story and they decided not to tell anyone what had happened. Helen Sue admitted to her friend that it was kind of exciting, but what she hated most was that when she finally got control of herself she was weak kneed and hassling like a tired puppy. She worried that if Bubba ever got wind of what happened, and that she was not really wanting to stop her Latin lover, Bubba Joe would be hurt, along with a certain Latin guy.

It is really hard for a southerner to go on vacation, because something always seems to happen.

Chapter Twenty Five
Going To The Army

Bubba Joe was one of the lucky ones who never had to go to the Army. Our government decided to quit drafting just before he became of age. Bubba said he was no better than anyone else to have to go, but he sure was happy to hear that they had eliminated the draft. However, Rafe McCutson was drafted and made a trip to Viet-Nam. He always looked down on Bubba for not being one of the guys who spent a hitch in Nam.

There have been a lot of Southern boys to be drafted and served their country and so with the North, East and West. It doesn't matter where you live Uncle Sam is going to get you if you are of age and the draft is active. America's boys have been a brave lot to have joined the military during wartime to help keep America free. I for one am very proud of them and ask God to keep them safe during their time serving their country. God Bless The American Solider!

I joined Uncle Sam's macho brigade so I could wear there green (olive drab) and brown uniform and have that macho look. When I put on my dress greens and went off post into the city, man was I sharp. All the girls in town followed me around and were crazy about me, I was never short of dates.

I didn't leave a girlfriend back home so I needed companionship, but I really never had problems with being alone. I always managed to keep me a girl friend with transportation. The big problem was most of them had cars and no matter how hard I looked I didn't find but one girl with a pick-up truck. I felt a lot more comfortable with her , it was almost like being back home. All my old girl friends back in Tennessee drove trucks. My most special girl I can remember in Tennessee drove a four-wheeled drive Chevy with a huge dinosaur painted on the front and both doors. Boy was she evermore a turn on, we would rare back in that Chevy and motor all over West Tennessee.

Her name was Nelda Sue Jorgenson and man was she pretty. She had long blonde hair, ruby red lips, nice size hips and penetrating eyes that could bore a hole through a railroad iron. She was a very affectionate girl too. It was always honey this and darling that, but I liked her a whole lot anyway.

All the guys who went to school with me laughed at me because I had to teach her to read and write, but she never went to school. The people at the school who gave those little qualification test reported that she was a little slow, but I thought she learned really quick. I even went further and taught her some things that she would not have learned in a classroom. Any way to make a long story short Nelda Sue finally went to college and come home and hung out a shingle. She is known as the best doctor in town now. Do you suppose the ones that were doing all the laughing are getting some pretty hard shots.

I took basic training at Fort Hood, Texas. Hood was a large training base and we got a lot of exercise force marching across the back forty. Sergeant Wilkens was our drill sergeant and a very nice person, but he could be awfully hard on you in training. He was an extremely good man and soft hearted and every time one of us would do some special for one of our fellow soliders he would get misty eyed.

There was a little Mexican boy who took basic with us named Martinez and his mother passed away while we were in basic. Martinez didn't have the money to go home for the funeral so we all chipped in what we could to get him a bus ticket home and back. Every one chipped in and we even thought that some of the non-commissioned officers may have put in a little as well.

Sergeant Wilkens pulled a foot locker out from the bunk and got upon it and made a long speech about compassion and unity. With tears flowing down his cheeks he told us how proud he was of us and how great a bunch of guys we were. They next day was back to the grind, the same ole loud yelling hard driving sergeant we knew in field training. From then on we knew what was in his heart and gave him our very best. We turned out to be the winning squad in the compant, another speech.

I went on then to AIT (advanced infantry training or second eight) taken at Aberdeen Proving Grounds at Baltimore Maryland. Man was Baltimore one more town, strictly a military man's town. It was probably the most dirtiest town I had ever graced the streets of. Yet, there was always something going on in Baltimore. It was probably the first place I was ever propositioned by another man.

Just for the record I was then an ASAP (straight american person) I am now an ASAP and I will always be an ASAP.

From there I was shipped to Mannheim, Germany. I was put on the USS Darby and in 9 days we docked in some little town in England. We were carried the rest of the way to Mannheim by rail. There I spent the next three years of my life that most of which I enjoyed, some I didn't. Alford Joe and I went into the Army together and we asked at the induction center in Memphis, Tennessee If we could remain together. They promised us dearly that we could spend the entire stay in the military together.

We enjoyed basic training together and then AIT together in Baltimore, but when that was over he went to the big island in

Hawaii and I went in the other direction to Mannheim. As we shook hands at Baltimore and prepared to part Alford Joe said,

"You know what, I believe those people in Memphis wwere lying to us. You are probably right I told him, but we may as well just drop the subject".

We didn't see each other again the rest of his three years in the Army. He was a lot smarter than I he stayed in three years and went home, I stayed in eight years. He was a photographer and I was an instructor.

Three years in Germany was a very nice tour of duty and I gotm to see a lot of Europe in my stay there. I made a lot of friends in Germany, most were females, but a few males as well. One I remember like it was yesterday because we got into a fight in a gasthaus. When I sobered up I looked him up and promised never to attack him again, because I didn't like the beating he gave me. I got sore a few times, but never lonely.

Two of my friends and I bought us a bicycle when we first reached Germany to travel with. Bicycles were a lot more affordable than cars and man did we need something affordable.

We didn't have the money to buy a car for the first year so we traveled by bike and enjoyed it until winter of course. Let me inform you that ice and bikes don't mix.

John Curtiss Henson sold his bike first and got himself a car, but I had already gotten lucky and found me a girlfriend with an automobile so I didn't really need one at the time. John Curtiss felt big riding around in his Volkswagon bug until my girl and I pulled up beside him in her Mercedes her ex-husband left her.

She had the car and I was getting a little dab of money from Uncle Sam, need I say more.

One day it hit me Alford Joe had not written me anything except to send me his address in Hawaii. Her sure must have been having a wonderful time on the big island. So I decided to write him, I wrote him twice and got no response whatsoever. A couple of months of me sending him mail finally got a card from some lady at his address saying that he was not going to be able to answer any of my letters, because he just didn't have the time.

I guess he was just too busy becoming a solider to write me a ten minute letter so I got the message and quit writing.

From there on I lost all contact with Alford Joe until we got home. He joked and told me about this wonderful lady he had met on the big island. He said the only real problem he had was to be sure that they didn't have any children, because thar was a real no-no in Hawaii and his lady would never be able to live with it. He also explained that the government did not give out welfare checks over there when unmarried women had children. He told me that women with three kids there had to have three jobs.and it really helped to hold down broken families and divorce.

When I left Europe I was shipped back to Fort Campbell, Kentucky for almost two years, then on to Viet-Nam. I spent one year in Viet-Nam and wasn't very crazy about it. Man was Nam evermore different from Europe. From the beautiful mountains and the Black Forest to rice paddys and mud. From cool sunshiny days to 140 degrees and rain, rain, rain. From long legged attractive blondes to dark brown brunettes, straw hats and slant eyes, not to mention the complexion. From English speaking darlings to short babbling pajama clad women. European women chewed on your ear and the Vietnamese women chewed on a ga-ga twig that turned their teeth black and looked like something a scientist would talk about. There was as much difference between the two countries as there is between yellow and red. When finally one day it was time to come home and even though it took quite sometime to do so I finally readjusted to our good ole Southern style living and I haven't been back to the Orient since and don't believe I will.

In some ways I missed a part of my military experience, but I felt honored to serve my country. I believe it to be the greatest place in the world to be, yet changes we are seeing are scaring me. The homeland people now seem to be slipping away from the original God fearing people that made America a great Nation, may God have mercy on those who are participating.

CHAPTER TWENTY SIX
Night Riders

In earlier Tennessee history there were a group of men who rode the hours of darkness and called themselves simply The Night Riders. They chilled the hearts of many citizens even though their purpose was not directed at the heartland residents.

The night riders manned themselves in 1907 and in the beginning they patrolled the Reelfoot Lake. Their main purpose was to maintain an arisen problem between the lakeshore settlers and rich property owners surrounding the lake.

The lake formed in 1811 by an earthquake was approximately 20 miles long and 7 miles wide at various points. It was a shallow lake, but the Mississippi River ran backwards for twenty four hours to fill the gorge. The large lake had taken an enormous amount of land away from the farming countryside so many chose or perhaps turned to fishing for their livelihood.

Reelfoot Lake got its name from an Indian prince whom had been born with one deformed foot. So badly deformed that he reeled when he walked. He had looked for an Indian princess to take as his wife, but could not find one who would have him in his condition. Giving up he turned to another tribe to find his bride to be. This was not permitted in his tribe so when he took his new bride neither of the two tribes would accept them.

The Night Riders were becoming notorious in their locale and people were coming to fear them and their actions. Many stories were told and credit given to the members of the clan, some were true and some weren't. As the stories go they were guilty of several crimes and some heinous, but records indicate that they were guilty of only two murders, yet they were accused of many.

As residents sat around their home fires at night discussing the events of the notorious group the stories became larger, longer and more numerous. It was added after many months of their shenanigans that they became bored and began to lend a hand in correcting a few of their local domestic problems. It appeared that too many innocent people were being hurt or tortured by the evil that consumes the heart of man under stress. It was a hard land at that time, but the extreme pressures of the times were used as a reason for men carrying things a bit too far, so The Night Riders illuminated.

The story was told about one happening that was accredited to the night riders. There was a young farmer that worked a few acres locally that was noted for being a bit high tempered. He married a neighboring young lady and they had a baby. The woman was well known for being a good woman and had some troubles with her husband when things began to turn bad. The daughter was six now and a beautiful little lady, but he became so mad a times that he would beat his wife in front of the child. He knew his wife would not leave him, because it would be almost impossible for her to make a living for the child. He treated her so terribly that it got out into the neighborhood.

One morning he harnessed his team of mules and went to the field as he did every day. On up into the morning he had to stop and go to the woods to use the bathroom and when he returned he found a group of branches tied to his plow handle with a note attached saying, "how would you like to have these used on your back until the blood comes", signed Night Riders. This went on for days on the plow, in the barn, on a nearby fence until the farmer was almost afraid to go out to work.

All of a sudden it stopped just as quickly as it had started and the farmer never mistreated his wife again. Several things were told that made it appear that the night riders were not as bad as they were made out to be.

A lawyer was hired by the farmers and settlers to support them legally and it was the contention of the riders to let the law handle the affair until the lawyer bought into the opposite side and the land grab. In return for his deceit he lost his life and it was accredited to the night riders. The courts tried reprimanding but could not succeed and dropped it.

One thing I haven't told yet is about a man that lost his most prize mule. He would feed the mule alone and curry him like he was a five hundred dollar mule. The old gentleman searched the countryside for his mule, but never did find the mule. The elderly gentleman was heart broken by the loss of his companion, so he just moped around as he had lost his best friend and maybe he had!

One day while sitting alone on his porch he heard a noise and looked up to find a man leading his mule into the yard. He jumped up and ran to his mule and threw his arms around it and carried on a loving conversation with it for five minutes. Then he turned to the man to thank him for bringing his mule home, but the man held up his hand and quieted him and began his speech.

Sir, I know I could pretend to have found your mule and you would have never known the difference until you were questioned by the right people. I sir stole that mule because I thought he was such a pretty animal. I wanted him so badly that I stole him since I didn't have the money to buy him, I am very sorry sir. The old farmer ask, I understand that sir but why did you bring him back.

You see, I went to feed him one morning in the stall where I kept him hidden and there was a note tied around his neck. The note said that if the mule wasn't returned today along with the truth, that I would have the hide stripped off my back in narrow strips. It was signed by the night riders and sir I surely don't want trouble with that bunch.

Many other stories brings the question to surface. Was The Night Riders as bad as their legend?

The Prayer

Dear father in heaven, as we come before you today in Prayer may we ask your infinite wisdom upon us? May this wisdom be used to help the world to see the love that you so generously pour out upon us. May it lead us to be able to make our brother realize that we are only your servants and that our mission here on earth is for the purpose of being instrumental toward the building of your kingdom.

Give us strength and knowledge that we might boldly approach the subject and the stamina to see it through. Help us Lord to keep in first place the thought and knowledge that any accomplishment is for you, not us.

Merciful Father take our hand, for we are but one meek man, one small country that wishes to assist our fellow Christian as you would have it be. Through our weaknesses Dear Father I have come to know that it is your strength that has brought us this far and that it will be your Love, your Strength, your Mercy and your Grace that will carry us further.

Forgive us Dear Father and have mercy upon us and our brother the world over.

In Jesus Name
Amen

ABOUT THE AUTHOR

The Author is a sixty-four year old male who advocates Christian living and the preparation of our children to follow in our footsteps.

Traveling half way around the world, visiting several foreign countries and more than half the states in our own great country, he has always come back to the South.

Practicing his desire to write this book with an early day and present day mixture, without being offensive he has labeled this book as Southern humor.

Born and educated in the great Volunteer state he completed his education at the University of Tennessee. He now offers his second book Crispy Fried And Southern Brown.

Printed in the United States
80094LV00004B/328-351